DECISION

That night, I tossed and turned a million times, hearing Charlotte's screams as those Indians surrounded her, wishing they had taken me instead of my sister.

All at once, I knew what I had to do. I got up and peeked through the door into the kitchen. Ma was asleep in her chair. I took one last look at her and slipped out the door.

By the time I caught Gray Back, the sky was good and light in the east. I climbed on him bareback and eased him out of the yard quiet-like, so Ma wouldn't hear me.

"Come on, old fellow," I told Gray Back as I climbed on him. "We're findin' Charlotte, and we ain't comin' back until we do."

AGAINST
A CROOKED SKY

Eleanor Lamb
and
Douglas Stewart

BANTAM BOOKS · LONDON
TORONTO · NEW YORK

☙

AGAINST A CROOKED SKY
A Bantam Book / April 1976

Published simultaneously in the United States and Canada

Bantam Books are published by Bantam Books, Inc. Its trade-
mark, consisting of the words "Bantam Books" and the por-
trayal of a bantam, is registered in the United States Patent
Office and in other countries. Marca Registrada. Bantam
Books, Inc., 666 Fifth Avenue, New York, New York 10019.

PRINTED IN THE UNITED STATES OF AMERICA

AGAINST
A CROOKED SKY

Chapter One

I remember like it was yesterday how those five Indians came riding out of nowhere right up to our cabin in the Black Ridge country. It was in the early 1850s, and I was only eleven, but I remember well how it all happened.

Pa was in Fort Williams buying planting seed, and Ma had just left with Milt Adams to see what she could do for his wife, Jenny. Ma was the best doctor in the homestead country, and when Milt came charging in with his team in a lather, all excited for fear Jenny had the cholera, Ma got her black bag from the shelf and went with him. But not before she gave me strict orders to mind Charlotte and not be up to my usual pranks.

It was like Ma knew without anyone telling her that down by the swimming hole in the pasture, a bit earlier, I'd stole Charlotte's clothes and put them on my pet calf for a joke. Callie looked right cute in my sister's pantaloons and her hair ribbon tied on one ear. Charlotte was some upset, but she couldn't do anything but holler, since she was swimming in her birthday clothes. She threatened to tell Pa when he came home, but she didn't know then she had little chance of ever seeing Pa again.

I remember standing on the porch watching Ma and Milt pull away from the cabin. When they were out of sight, I got a tight feeling in my chest, wondering what would become of Ma if she got the cholera from Jenny. I turned to Charlotte, who was inspecting her pantaloons.

1

"Don't think you're gettin' away with what you did, Sam Isaac Sutter," she said, reminding me again. "You'll get your just dues when Pa gets home."

"What about Ma?" I asked, ignoring her. "Won't she git the cholera, too?"

"Maybe," she said.

When she didn't show much concern, I looked at her, startled.

"But she'll die!"

"You don't think that would stop her from goin', do you? Ma wouldn't take a thought to her own life if she could help to save Jenny's."

"But that don't make sense," I complained, ". . . Ma dyin' to save Jenny."

"She ain't gonna die," she said as she went inside.

I followed her in. "Well, she could!"

"There's more to it than that, Sam, and a lot you don't understand. If a person's everything he should be, he won't be thinkin' of himself first . . . even if it means dyin'.'"

I thought my sister had gone plumb crazy. "Where'd ya ever git that idea?"

She motioned to the Bible on the sideboard. "Right under your nose, silly . . . the Holy Scriptures."

I snorted and went to get a loaf of bread from the cupboard, where Ma always kept it in a big lard can.

"That's right," insisted Charlotte. "It says right there in the Bible . . . you can't have any greater love than to give your life for a friend."

I pondered what she'd said for a minute while I got a knife from the cupboard drawer and sliced me some bread, then I said, "I don't know anybody I'd die for."

She went to the sideboard and picked up the Bible and stood by the window thumbing through it. My sister was near sixteen and sure enough pretty, but when she talked about things in that book, her face lit up like a candle in the dark.

I put some elderberry jam on my bread and took a bite. "Would you die for me, Charlotte?"

Startled, she gazed at me for a bit. "I'd die for anyone in our family, Sam," she said. Then her eyes took on a teasing look. "And I'm sorry to say . . . that includes you."

I grinned at her, knowing by the way she said it she wasn't mad at me anymore for what I'd done down by the swimming hole. All at once I saw her stiffen as something caught her eye outside of the window. I could tell what she saw scared the Scriptures right out of her.

"Sam!" she gasped out. "Come and look! Quick!"

I hurried over, and what she was looking at made my knees go weak as water.

"Injuns!" I gasped.

Charlotte didn't say anything, but just stared like she was in some kind of a trance.

"I ain't never seen no Injuns like them before!" I exclaimed as I gaped beside Charlotte.

The only clothes they had on was some sort of loincloth made of real fancy material. They had bracelets on their arms, and funny looking moccasins that were cut out at the toes and laced up their legs with a fringe on top. The leader wore a gold headband that glinted in the sun. He put me in mind of a noble prince riding out of the past with his knights of old. They rode right toward our cabin, looking straight ahead, and I couldn't get my eyes unglued from them.

"Charlotte!" I finally gasped, ". . . what'll we do?"

Dropping the Bible into her pocket, she backed away from the window and rushed over to the door, sliding the heavy bolt across it. I looked at her, then at the Indians, too scared to move. She jerked the heavy table from its place over the large braided rug covering the trapdoor that led into the root cellar.

"Sam!" she yelled.

I finally got my legs working, but not before I took one last look at the Indians. They were almost to the cabin, and Charlotte was struggling with the trapdoor.

"Sam! Get over here and help!"

I got there in a hurry, and with both of us tugging on it, we finally got it open enough for Charlotte to get through to the narrow stairway beneath. She held the door for me, but before climbing in, I had to take one last look, certain I'd see an Indian's face staring through the window.

"Sam!"

Charlotte's voice brought me scurrying through the opening. Then she dropped the door. The cellar was so black I could hardly find my way to the bottom of the stairs. We crouched in the corner, our eyes glued to the little slivers of light that leaked through the cracks around the trapdoor.

It was the first time we'd ever had to hide from anybody, and we didn't know what to expect. About that time, the cabin door rattled like a keg of horseshoes rolling down a hill. My heart pushed up in my throat until I thought it would strangle me.

"Charlotte!" I gasped, "what if they find the trapdoor?"

The door rattled again, much louder this time, then all was quiet. A big pine pole supported the floor of the cabin, and my sister grabbed a small coil of rope that hung on it and tied the trapdoor to the pole. We listened but couldn't hear a sound.

"Maybe they've gone," I whispered.

"You can bet they haven't," said Charlotte.

Then I had an awful thought. "They'll git Callie!" I said.

"Hush!"

"But I don't want them—"

A loud crash from above cut me off as they broke the cabin window.

"Oh! . . . they're comin' in!" I gasped.

Charlotte's hand clamped over my mouth. "Will you be still!"

The floor creaked overhead as footsteps moved across it.

"They'll scalp us for sure!" I whimpered. "I wish Pa'd come home."

Charlotte shook me good. "Hush up, Sam. You start bawling—"

The trapdoor jerking up and down cut her off, and my stomach turned inside out. From the slivers of light coming from above, I saw Charlotte's face turn the color of Ma's bread dough. She put her arm around me and pulled me close to her as we huddled there in the dark. I could feel her body trembling against mine, and we watched in terror as the rope on the pole began to slip.

"Come on!" she said, leaping to her feet. "We've got to use the tunnel! It's our only chance!"

She didn't have to tell me twice, and we felt our way to the corner of the cellar. The walls were crawly with cobwebs and spiders and all kinds of bugs, but we scraped them away from the door that was almost completely hidden. Charlotte slid the bolt back and tried to pull the door open. It was swelled up from the dampness of the cellar, and the hinges were rusted. It wouldn't budge. I looked up

5

at the trapdoor and almost hollered when I saw the eyes of an Indian brave peering down into the cellar. I felt Charlotte freeze and suck in her breath.

"Please, God," she whispered, "we need your help. We've got to get out of here!"

We tugged some more, then all at once the door flew open just like someone had lambasted it from the other side. I scrambled into the small, crawly tunnel. I had to wiggle and squirm to move along and wondered if Charlotte could make it since she was bigger than me. I wasn't long getting to the light at the other end, but I was careful about poking my head out. I could almost feel an Indian's tomahawk splitting my skull. After seeing it was safe, I climbed out with Charlotte right after me.

Any other time I'd have died laughing at her, she was so covered with dirt and trash. If she'd have known her hair was full of cobwebs and bugs, she'd have screeched her head off.

She grabbed my hand, and we sneaked through the low bushes that lined the yard until we came to the haystack. We kept that between us and the cabin as we headed for the corral. Then I spotted Callie! She was laying asleep in the shade, and I pulled up short. Charlotte gave me a hard jerk.

"Come on!" she scolded me.

"But they'll git her for sure!"

"We can't be worryin' about that calf!"

"We could take her with us," I argued.

"On Gray Back? Don't be silly. He'll have trouble enough carryin' both of us."

I felt like a big rock had been tied to my heart. I loved Callie. Pa had given her to me for my very own after a mountain lion had killed her ma, and I wasn't about to leave her for no Indians. I kept pulling back, but Charlotte dragged me along the pole fence to the corral where our horse, Gray Back, stood like he was waiting for us. Charlotte took the bridle from the gate and put it on him. She swung up on his back, and all the while, I couldn't keep my eyes off of my calf.

"Hurry up . . . get on!" ordered Charlotte when she saw me hesitate.

I looked back at the cabin, then at Callie. I couldn't stand it any longer.

"I ain't leavin' her!" I declared. "Not for them Injuns!"

I turned and ran toward the haystack with Charlotte yelling right after me.

"Sam! No! Get back here!"

She whirled Gray Back and followed me. I tried to dart away from her, but she was faster than me and slid off and grabbed me with both hands. I got a good shaking.

"When will you ever learn to mind, Sam Isaac?" she scolded.

"Please, Charlotte," I begged. "We can't leave Callie for them Injuns!"

Then I guess she could see how much I loved my calf, and she said, "Oh, all right, but you're goin' to get us caught yet."

I ran to Callie and lifted her to her feet. Charlotte helped me shove her into some bushes at the side of the barnyard. We tied her up with a short piece of rope I always kept around Callie's neck.

"They won't look for her there," she told me. "Now, let's get out of here!"

I legged her up on Gray Back in a hurry, and she pulled me up behind her. She had him in a gallop almost before I was ready. I looked back just in time to see the Indians dashing out of the cabin toward their ponies.

"They're comin'!" I screeched, and Charlotte went to whipping Gray Back.

I held on like a wood tick, knowing we were headed for the Adams' homestead. I looked over my shoulder again.

"They're gainin' on us, Charlotte!" I hollered, the wind whipping my words away. "We ain't gonna make it!"

Charlotte chanced a look and cried, "We'll make it!"

She turned Gray Back off the road and headed him cross-country. She was on the shortcut to the Adams' place. Old Gray Back was pounding like his life depended on it, and the Indians began to fall back. We were doing all right until we came to that deep gully. Our horse checked for a second, then lunged so hard to clear it we both flipped off, landing in the dirt.

I scrambled to my feet and took one quick look at the Indians. They were still coming. I rushed to Charlotte as she tried to get to her feet. I could see she was hurt bad. Her face was twisted with pain, and she tried not to cry. I tugged at her.

"Charlotte," I pleaded. "Get up!"

"I can't," she whimpered. "My leg's hurt!"

I tried to lift her, and she stumbled to her feet. I ran for Gray Back who had stopped a few feet away. By this time, the Indians were almost upon us.

"Quick, Sam!" Charlotte cried, "Get on and ride!"

"What about you! I—I can't leave you!"

"Do as I say! Go for help!"

She helped to boost me on the horse then slapped him on the rump. I kicked him into a full run. I topped the rise of a hill and looked back to see Charlotte hopping like a crippled rabbit toward the nearest clump of scrub oak. Then the Indians surrounded her in a cloud of dust. I knew there was nothing I could do but get to the Adams' homestead as fast as I could.

A few minutes later, I clattered into their place yelling, at the top of my voice. Milt and Ma came running from the house, and Jeb and Matt, Milt's two grown sons, rushed from the barn where they were stacking hay. My breath was so near gone when I slid off my horse, I could hardly sob out my story to them. Ma's face took on a look of horror and unbelief, and she turned away. Milt ordered his boys to saddle some horses while he went to the house for his gun.

"Stay with your ma until we git back!" he ordered me, as they rode off at a fast gallop in the direction from which I had come.

I looked at Ma wanting to comfort her, but didn't know how to go about it.

"Charlotte made me leave 'er," I told Ma in a hurry. "If I hadn't, they'd have got us both."

Ma's face turned as gray as the winter's sky.

"I hate them redskins!" she said bitterly, "I—I—" Then her shoulders began to shake, and she started to cry. That was something I'd never seen Ma do before, and I remember how awful it made me feel. It must have showed on my face, because she reached out and pulled me to her and went right on crying.

Chapter Two

Jenny didn't have the cholera after all, and when Milt came home with no news of Charlotte, she insisted he take me and Ma home.

It was almost dark before Pa got back from Fort Williams. I sat in the corner of our kitchen watching Ma rocking in her chair, a look of despair on her face. I kept trying to talk to her, but she seemed to be off in another world. She'd quit crying, though, and I was glad about that.

I perked up when I heard Pa coming into the yard with his team and wagon. I knew it was him by the way he talked to his horses.

"Pa's home!" I cried, running to the window to look out.

I saw his shadowy figure leap from the wagon, and he headed straight for the cabin. Ma slowly got to her feet. Pa busted through the door, and I knew by the look on his face he'd already heard what had happened.

Pa just being there did something to Ma. He put his arms around her and held her tight against him. I guess that was the kind of comforting she'd needed all the time.

"Mollie . . . Mollie," he said as Ma went to crying harder. "Try not to take on so."

"Thank heaven they found you!" she could hardly get the words out. "Oh, John . . . do somethin'."

Pa's face became dark as a river bottom at midnight. He crossed to the fireplace and slid out some bricks that covered his cache of ammunition. He took out a good supply, then turned back to Ma.

"If they've done anythin' to her—!"

He didn't finish, but from the way he looked, I wouldn't have wanted to be those Indians when he did find them. I went over to him.

"Let me go with you, Pa," I said.

"No, Sam," said Pa. "I want you here with your ma."

"But don't you see . . . I've gotta go! It's all my fault they got Charlotte."

"Now, there's no need of blamin' yourself," Ma said, wiping her eyes with her apron.

"If I hadn't gone back for Callie—"

There was a dead silence, and Pa stared at me. "You what!"

I ducked my head, feeling more guilty than ever. I looked at Ma for help.

"They'd have got her, Ma!" I said. "I couldn't let 'em do that!"

"Yes," she said, turning away, an awful look on her face, ". . . And now they've got your sister."

I couldn't stand anymore, and rushed through the door to my bedroom. I threw myself on the bed. I couldn't hold back the tears even when I heard Pa say, "You mustn't blame the boy, Mollie."

"But goin' back for that calf . . . ," Ma said. "I shoulda never left 'em alone. You've gotta find her, John. You've just got to!"

"I will, Mollie," promised Pa, then yelled at me. "Sam, put up the team and be sure you feed 'em good."

I heard him leave, and in a few minutes I got up and went to the window. Pa was getting on his horse, and I watched until he rode out of sight.

That night, I tossed and turned a million times,

hearing Charlotte's screams as those Indians surrounded her. My imagination took off with me, and I could see all sorts of things happening to her. I thought she was staked out in a cactus bed, her skin parched and bleeding, her tongue thick and swollen from thirst. Then I'd see her buried alive in the sand with only her head and neck sticking out as wolves and coyotes snapping at her. I even imagined she was tied to a tree with squaws and Indian kids spitting on her or tormenting her with pointed sticks.

I turned my face into the pillow and tried to shut out these awful thoughts, wishing the Indians had taken me instead of my sister.

All at once, I knew what I had to do. I got up and peeked through the door into the kitchen. Ma was asleep in her chair. I sneaked to the cupboard and got two cold biscuits and put them in my shirt pocket. I took one last look at Ma and slipped out of the door. By the time I caught Gray Back, the sky was good and light in the east. I climbed on him bareback and eased him out of the yard quiet-like, so Ma wouldn't hear me. When I got a safe distance from the house, I put him to a gallop and headed for the place where the Indians had captured Charlotte. When I got there, the sun was almost up. The wind was rising with it, blowing dirt in the tracks the Indians had made. I could see the way the tracks were churned up that Pa and the homesteaders had been this way. Then something caught my eye. The sun, peeking over the mountain, glinted on the tip of an object lying in the sand. I slid off my horse and dropped to my knees, digging it out, then gaped. There was no mistaking it. It was the gold headband the Indian leader wore. Charlotte must have put up an awful fight before they took her. I turned it over and over in my hand, wiping the dust off. Engraved on it was an arrow

12

with a crooked shaft like a lightning bolt. I ran my belt through it and let it dangle from my waist.

"Come on, old fellow," I told Gray Back as I climbed on him. "We're findin' Charlotte, and we ain't comin' back 'til we do."

The tracks all led north, and I follered them for a while, having a heck of a time reading them. They went every which way, and I finally gave up and took out the way I figured I would go if I were those Indians.

I climbed hills and rode down gullies, and soon I was going through timber so thick I couldn't see any way I looked. I'd never been this far from home before. I guided Gray Back to the top of a high ridge and looked back toward the southwest. Nothing looked familiar. I was sure enough lost! I studied the country I'd come over; at the big black clouds gathering in the west. The air was getting cold and damp. I put my heels to my horse and headed down the slope. It wasn't long until rain started to fall, and soon I was soaked to the skin. I was so cold, my teeth chattered like a magpie in a summer peach tree, and I clamped my jaws tight to keep them from clicking. I looked for the sun, wondering what time it was, but the clouds had covered it. The rain soon became just a drizzle, but I was near froze by that time. All at once, the world seemed big and wide and lonely, and I wished Pa was with me. I felt a scare inside of my belly and wondered what I was going to do. Then I remembered how Charlotte was always reminding me about my prayers, and I wondered if God would take time out to help me now. I sure needed Him.

I slid off my horse and got down on my knees beside a big rock. I found it hard to ask God the things I wanted to, so I just talked to him the way I would my pa. When I got to my feet, I felt better and took out one of the biscuits from my shirt pocket. The other one I'd save for Charlotte. While I ate mine, I climbed back on my horse and rode on up the trail. The farther I went, the rougher it got, but I knew I had to go on. There was no way I could find my way back home, since the rain had washed out my tracks. It would be dark before long, then I'd have to hole up until morning. All at once, through the trees, I could see a big stream of water. It was a wide river, and I knew it had to be old Smoky I'd heard Pa talk about. On the other side of the river, I saw a cabin. I wanted to holler for joy when I saw smoke coming out of the chimney. I knew somebody was over there, and right then, I didn't care who.

About that time, Gray Back got a whiff of the water, and that's all it took to get him into a fast trot. I let him have his head, and we were there in a jiffy. While he drank his fill, I sized up the river. I didn't know much about fording a river as big as this one, but I could tell it wasn't going to be easy. I guess old Gray Back felt the same way, 'cause when I tried to ride him into it, he downright refused to go. I swatted him good with the reins, and he decided I was boss.

The river was a lot deeper than it looked, and it was muddy and swollen from the rain. It was sure a lot swifter than I thought, too, and we hadn't got out very far before Gray Back had to swim. The scary dark water made me dizzy, but it was too late to turn back. Gray Back was having trouble making any headway.

"Come on, Gray Back!" I hollered at him. "Swim! Swim!"

He snorted and blew his nose, then got down to the business of pushing himself through the current. It was soon easy to see he wasn't going to make it carrying my weight. I slid off on his downstream side, hanging on to his mane with one hand and swimming with the other. My body was soon so numb from the cold water, I could hardly use my legs. It was hard to keep up with him, and the river seemed to get wider and wider. When we got close enough to the other side, Gray Back's hoofs struck bottom, and he began lunging for the bank like he was trying to get away from a cougar. He broke my hold on his mane and flipped me back into the deep water. I yelled and grabbed for him, but it was too late. My head seemed to explode as a heavy piece of driftwood hit me. I sank beneath the surface then rose and sank again. My mouth and lungs filled with water. Gagging and choking, I tried to clear my brain. I was sure I was dying. Then, from far off, I thought I heard someone holler as the water sucked me under. I came up again and a voice bellered out, "Dadburn it, kid! Git hold of that rope!"

My strength was almost gone, but I could see a blurry, hairy shape moving toward me through the water. In that instant, I saw it was a big dog with a rope in his mouth.

"Grab it, boy! Grab it, I say!" the voice boomed out again.

I tried to do as I was told, but missed. I tried it again. Then something hard filled my hands and I clung on with all I had. I felt myself being pulled through the water and up the bank. The last thing I remember hearing was the barking of a dog, before everything went black.

Chapter Three

When I opened my eyes, things looked hazy at first, then finally got clearer. I was lying on a homemade cot in a one-room log cabin. I was all bundled up in an Indian blanket while my clothes hung over a chair in front of the fireplace to dry. The biggest man I'd ever seen sat across from me slouched down in a chair made out of some kind of small poles. He had a heavy beard and long hair and stared at me from eyes as hard as Pa's anvil. A half-empty whiskey jug moved up and down on his belly with every breath. A huge, shaggy dog lay on the floor at his feet, his head on his paws, watching me.

I pulled the blanket tighter around me and tried not to look at the man. He kept staring at me and didn't say a word for a long time. I was so scared, for a bit, I almost wished I'd drowned in the river.

"Where'd you come from?" His deep voice came out so sudden it made me jump.

When I didn't say anything, he got louder. "Well, speak up! What's your name?"

I still wouldn't answer, and the big dog came over to me and started licking my face. I tried to hit him, thinking he was maybe going to eat me up. The man laughed, but I didn't see anything funny about it.

"He saved your life, boy!" he said. "And he's jest tryin' to make you welcome."

Just as if the feller had told him to do it, the dog jumped up on me and began to maul me. I shoved at him, trying to get out of his way.

"Git outta here" I yelled.

"See there!" the man said, still laughing. "He likes you. He likes you real good."

No matter how I tried to get away from the dog, he kept at me.

Finally, the man yelled, "Killer, git over here! Right now, or I'll shoot ya!"

The dog left me and went over to him, and the man ruffled his head with his big hand like he sure loved him.

"Ol' B'ar Killer wouldn't kill nobudy but b'ars and Injuns . . . and maybe a white kid or two."

I gulped and nearly pulled the blanket over my head when he gave the dog a sharp kick with the side of his boot and said, "Now, git over there where you belong!"

The dog whimpered then sneaked over to the corner of the cabin and lay down, looking like he sure enough had his feelings hurt. I didn't feel too good myself, wondering what kind of feller I'd come up against. I looked at the dog, then at the bearded man as he raised his jug of booze to his mouth and took a long pull. He slouched deeper in his chair and gazed at me with a heavy scowl on his face.

"You don't know who I am, do ya?" he asked.

I shook my head.

"Well, folks call me Russian. Russian Habbakuk. You know . . . I had a son like you once, only he was ugly as dirt. Took after 'is ma."

He took a knife from the inside of his boot and rolled its shiny blade in the light of the fire, then went on, "I ended up havin' to cut 'is throat."

I guess my eyes most jumped out of my head, and I shoved myself back further on the cot as close to the wall as I could. Russian laughed again, knowing he was scaring the gizzard right out of me.

"Who are ya, anyway?"

17

I couldn't force out a word.

"Speak up, boy!" he boomed out, and I jumped like he'd stabbed me with a hot poker.

"S-Sam S-Sutter," I stammered.

"You one of them Mormons from the Black Ridge country?"

I nodded, then getting up my courage, I said, "I'm lookin' for my sister. She was stole by Injuns, and I ain't turnin' back until I find 'er."

"Well, now! Ain't you a gritty one." He snickered. "Hear that, Killer? This li'l boy cain't even ford a river or pack a gun, and he's off in b'ar and Injun country alone. Not even a saddle or a grub bag. What do you expect ta live on? What you got in your pockets?"

He reached down in a pile of skins on the floor beside him and pulled out my gold headband. ". . . Or maybe this purty li'l trinket, here?"

I came off the bed, clutching my blanket around me, and flew at him, forgetting how scared I was.

"Give me that! It's mine!" I yelled.

Russian put out his hand to hold me off and lifted the headband out of my reach.

"So it's yours, is it? Well, now . . . why don't you take it?"

He shoved the band toward me, and I made a grab for it. He jerked it out of my reach again.

"That's mine! Now give it here!"

"I said, take it," he taunted.

I made a grab for it again, and he raised it above his head. Real mad now, I slammed against him and went to slugging him with my fists. The next thing I knew, I was lying on the floor, and B'ar Killer stood over me, his teeth showing in an ugly snarl. Russian gave the dog a quick kick.

"Git, ya scraggy mongrel," he said.

B'ar Killer yelped and slinked over to the corner

again. Still hanging on to my blanket, I got back to my feet. I couldn't figure out what was going on between this man and dog.

Russian chuckled. "He likes you all right, but he likes me better." Then he flourished the headband. "Now, where'd you git this?"

"I found it," I said. "It's off one of them Injuns that stole my sister."

"Found it, did you? Well, I ain't seen nothin' like this off no Injun. King of Siam, maybe, but no Injun." He sniffed at the band. "Hell, it don't even smell like an Injun, and there ain't nobudy that knows 'em better'n me." He put the band on his head. "Ha! It jest fits."

I was so mad I was ready to come loose from my britches again, and he started to laugh and walked over to the fireplace.

"Does your ma 'n' pa know you're here?" he asked.

"No," I said.

He lifted a kettle of steaming stew from the fire to the hearth and said, "There's one thing you got, Sam Sutter, and thet's guts!"

I glared at him as he took a wooden spoon from where it hung on the side of the fireplace. Turning back to me, he brandished it.

"But there's ones thing ya ain't got, and thet's know-how!"

My eyes went back to the kettle of stew, and my stomach sort of turned over. B'ar Killer stood with his head in it, lapping it up like he thought it was all his. Russian shoved him out of the way while he ladled some stew into two bowls. The dog came back for more, and Russian booted him with the side of his foot.

"Git away!" he growled. "You've had your share. There's others of us."

19

Licking his chops, B'ar Killer went to his corner to lay down, looking with sorrowful eyes first at Russian, then at me.

Russian carried the bowls of stew to the table and set one in front of me, still talking, "Why, I've been trappin' up 'n' down the Ol' Smoky for nigh onta thirty years. I know every tribe from here to the divide. Speak six Injun tongues and still have to hang onto my scalp. And here a runt like you comes bargin' into grizzly country without as much as a gun or enough sense to cross a river where it's wide."

He sat down at the table and began to slurp his food. I watched him for a minute, wondering how I was going to get up the courage to eat mine—even as hungry as I was. He stopped to lick his lips and looked at me.

"Well . . . what's the matter? Eat up!"

"I don't want none," I said, my eyes going quickly to B'ar Killer. Russian snatched his knife from the table and gripped it in his big fist.

"Turn my stew down, will ya!" he yelled. "You know what I've a mind to do? Slit your throat!"

It didn't take me long to start shoveling in the stew. I shut my eyes and pretended I didn't see B'ar Killer, his hurt forgotten, back eating from the kettle again. Russian set his knife down and gazed at first me then the dog.

"Aw, don't mind him," he said. "You won't find no cleaner hound in all this territory."

I gagged a little and couldn't help but pull a face as I tried to force the food down.

"Why, you little chicken liver!" he hollered. "Insult my dog, will ya!"

I kept at it until I emptied the bowl, and when I looked up again, Russian had taken the gold band from his head and was examining it.

"No, sir," he said. "In all my years of dealin' with redskins, I ain't never seen nothin' like this before. I bet it's worth somethin'. Probably two or three hundred dollars. I'd have to trap for three or four years to git that kind of money."

"Well, you can't have it," I told him.

He ignored me. "There ain't nothing purtier than sweet, yeller gold."

He put the band back on his head and belched loud enough to make the windows rattle, then patted his belly. He threw me a bearskin that hung over the back of his chair.

"Here's your bed, runt," he said, heading for his cot in the corner, "and I ain't about to say another word to you 'til mornin', when I take you back home."

"Home? I ain't goin' home!"

"Now, ain't you?" He sat down on the cot to pull off his boots. I got brave and went over to stand in front of him.

"I tell ya, I ain't goin' back! Not 'til I find my sister, and you can't make me! Now you give me what's mine, and I'll be off!"

He took the gold band from his head and, chuckling to himself, stuffed it under his pillow.

"I tell ya, I ain't goin' home!" I said again, louder this time.

He pulled off his shirt. "Sure you are. Ask ol' B'ar Killer there if I won't take ya. Ain't that right, Killer? Sure 'tis!"

B'ar Killer came trotting over to Russian as the trapper took a jug from under the bed and uncorked it. He slurped a good slug of booze, then flopped back on his cot. Patting his dog's head, he turned out the lantern. I sulked in front of the fire for a while with half of a mind to land right in the middle of him and try to wrassle my headband away. I got rid of that idea in a hurry when old B'ar Killer planted himself right down by the side of Russian like he planned on staying in that spot for the rest of the night.

Chapter Four

That old Russian! If he wasn't something else. The next morning, we were headed back to the homestead just like he said, and there wasn't any way I could talk him out of it. Once I made a run for my horse to try to get away, but he pounced on me like a bear would a trout in a shallow stream and shook me good.

"Ya little rascal!" he scolded me. "I said I was takin' ya home, and that's what I'm doin'. Now, you can go decent like, or I'll tie you to that horse. You've got your choice."

I was so all-fired mad at him, I couldn't talk back, but I knew there was no use to try pulling that again.

By midafternoon, we were riding across the meadow toward our cabin, Russian singing at the top of his voice and drinking out of that whiskey jug he'd brought along. B'ar Killer followed behind him, looking up at him now and again like he was real proud of the way his master was carrying on. We spotted Ma watching us from the cabin porch. Russian took another slug of booze, then kept on with his singing:

> "Oh, yes, oh, my! You're soon gonna cry!
> 'Cause you'll git a right good strappin'!
> As sure as hell, it's gonna happen!"

"Shhhh!" I warned him. "Ma don't take kindly to drunks!"

"Drunks!" he roared. "I ain't no drunk, am I B'ar Killer?"

He tipped his bottle of booze and let it run to-

23

ward the ground. Before I could say bread and butter, B'ar Killer was right up there lapping it out of the air. I stared wide-eyed, and Russian almost fell off his horse, laughing. B'ar Killer licked his chops and looked up at Russian begging for more.

"That's your share," Russian told him. "I ain't wastin' no more good whiskey on a hound like you. Now, git back where you belong."

B'ar Killer went back to foller behind Russian's horse again. Ma watched us from the porch, looking more tired and worried than I'd ever seen her, but I could tell she was relieved to see me. She wasn't too taken in with Russian and his antics, though. When we stopped our horses in front of the cabin, he tipped his hat.

"Afternoon, ma'am," he said, then hiccuped. "My name's Habbakuk, but folks jist call me Russian. You mighta heered of me. I've trapped in these parts nigh onto thirty years now."

Ma nodded at him, then got on me good. "Where've you been, Sam Isaac? Ain't we got enough trouble without you runnin' off?"

"I found your little runt near drowned in the Ol' Smoky," said Russian before I could get a word in, "but me an' B'ar Killer drug 'im out and brung 'im back to you, didn't we, ol' boy?"

B'ar Killer wagged his tail and whined like he was sure glad to get his share of the glory.

"Ma," I put in as quick as I could, "have they found Charlotte yet?"

Russian gave me a disgusted look. "You don't see 'er dancin' no jig, now, do ya?" He turned to Ma. "If I was you, ma'am, I'd give this boy a lickin' . . . a right good one, too."

The way Ma's face twisted, I knew she was chuck full of misery.

24

"I thank you for bringin' him back, Mr. Habbakuk," she managed, then turned to me and choked out, "but Sam, I—I just can't take anymore! I can't!" Then she turned and rushed into the cabin.

"Ma!" I cried out, sliding from my horse to foller her. "Wait, I—" I turned to Russian, hoping he would help me out, but he just squinted down at me.

"Go on. Git in there," he said, "and take what's comin' to ya. An' next time, leave the searchin' to men. Come on, Killer."

He turned his horse to ride away, B'ar Killer at his heels. He was a good piece away when I took after him on the run.

"Hey! Wait!" I yelled. "You've got my headband!"

Russian either didn't hear me or paid me no nevermind, for he went to singing at the top of his voice. I trotted up beside his horse.

"I want my headband!" I hollered again.

Russian looked down at me and went right on. "It ain't gonna do you no good," he jeered, ". . . and I jist think I'll keep it."

I was some full of mad by this time. "You give it here!" I yelled. Russian glared down at me, then took the gold headband from his saddlebag. He rubbed his hand over it like he was petting B'ar Killer.

"Gold," he said. "That's what it is. Sweet, yeller gold! Tain't no use to a kid, noways."

He started to put it back in his saddlebag, and I snatched at it. He jerked it out of my reach.

"You ain't havin' it!" I yelled. "It's mine!"

"Why, you ungrateful brat!" he snorted. "We shoulda let you drown in the river . . . huh, Killer?"

He looked at me hard for a minute, then in disgust threw the headband down on the ground. I

25

grabbed it up and put it behind my back, daring him to try to take it away from me, but he just laughed and, kicking his mule, went off singing at the top of his voice.

I watched him for a bit, then headed back toward the cabin. I looked down at the headband, then polished it on my pants leg. The way it shone in the sun, I decided it was about the prettiest thing I'd ever seen, excepting maybe for Charlotte, and thinking of her sure made me wish my pa would come home.

It was a couple of days later before he did, though, and Ma had plenty of time to get after me for running off. She spent most of her time on the porch watching the hills for some sign of Pa. When we finally saw him coming with Milt and the other homesteaders, we ran a good way out to meet them. When we got close, we could see Charlotte wasn't with them.

"Did ya find 'er, Pa?" I hollered out anyway. "Did ya find Charlotte?"

Ma didn't wait for his answer but just headed back for the cabin, her shoulders sagging like she carried a thirty-pound bucket of water in each hand.

Pa nor any of the homesteaders had much to say until they pulled up in front of the house, and I told Pa where I'd been. He was some put out with me until I showed him the headband. He took it for a good look.

"Where'd ya get this, Sam?"

I told him, and he handed it to Milt. "What do ya think of it?" he asked.

Milt studied it, then passed it on to the others.

"There ain't no way a' knowin' for sure if it even come off an Injun," he said.

"It sure did," I put in. "I found it right where he got Charlotte."

The homesteaders exchanged glances, then wearily looked at Pa. He squinted at them, and I noticed how tired he looked.

"Now see here, fellers," he said. "I ain't expectin' you to go out with me again. You've given enough of your time, already."

"There ain't really no place left to look, John," said Milt. "We've covered near all the territory for miles around, and I should be gittin' back ta Jenny, her bein' sick an' all."

Dade Connely, the last homesteader to look at the headband, shifted his weight uneasily in the saddle as Pa took it back from him.

"I'd sure like to go on with you, John," he said, "but—"

Pa cut him off. "I'm obliged ta all of you for what you've done, and I ain't likely to forget it."

He shook hands with them all, and Milt was the last to leave. Ma looked up at Pa from where she stood on the porch, her face pinched with hurt.

"You ain't givin' up, are you, John?" she asked.

"I ain't gonna quit 'til I find 'er, Mollie," he said, "so don't you worry."

Ma kind of sobbed and hurried into the cabin. Pa and me both gazed after her for a minute, then I said, "I'll go with you, Pa. We don't need nobudy else to find Charlotte."

Pa went to his horse and put the headband in his saddlebag.

"There ain't no way, son," he said, picking up his horse's reins and heading for the corral.

I follered right behind. "Please, Pa," I pleaded. "I've gotta help find 'er, 'cause I'm to blame—"

27

"Look, Sam," Pa cut me off. "You did wrong goin' off before. This time, I expect you to stay here and take care of your ma and look after things. I'm dependin' on you, son."

"Yeah, Pa," I said, my voice getting all tight from the lump in my throat. "If that's what ya want."

The next morning, Ma and me stood on the front porch and watched Pa ride away leading his pack-mule. He looked awful lonesome going off alone like that, and when he got to the top of the hill he turned and waved, and I felt empty inside. I looked up at Ma, and she had tears in her eyes.

"He'll find 'er, Ma." I tried to comfort her. "He'll come back with her ridin' right behind him. You'll see."

But weeks went by, and Pa didn't come home. I kept fresh meat on the table, the chores done and the corn hoed. With Ma's help, I even put up the hay in the little meadow. When fall came, and the leaves started turning yellow, I knew Pa hadn't found Charlotte yet, and maybe wouldn't be back 'til winter. I watched the geese flying south and Ma's anxious looks toward the pass in the hills where Pa should come riding through. Many times, I heard her sobbing in the night. I knew she cried for Charlotte and Pa, too, and I couldn't help but feel guilty, knowing I was to blame for it all.

Chapter Five

When Pa finally did come home, winter had set in, but he hadn't found any trace of Charlotte. He got back before the first hard snow hit, and it didn't take long for the mountain passes to clog so he couldn't go out again. He told us he'd follered every rumor he'd ever heard of, and so far there'd been nothing to give him hope.

"But I'll find 'er come spring, Mollie," he said. "If she's alive, I'll find 'er."

Ma didn't say anything, but just leaned against him and cried. That night I dreamed about my sister on a hill, the wind whipping her dress and hair. She kept beckoning to me, and when I'd get close she'd be gone. Then all at once, she appeared farther on, still beckoning. I woke up in a cold sweat, wondering why I would dream such a thing.

Winter finally broke, and the melting snow ran through our barnyard and into the pond we used for summer irrigation. Pa and I stood side by side watching it fill. He turned to me.

"I'll be goin' after Charlotte again, Sam," he said. "Right soon now."

"Please, Pa," I said. "Let me go with you."

He looked off over the hills and put his arm across my shoulders. "I need you to carry on for me here, son. There's corn to plant and wood to cut, and all them chores to keep you busy. It's too much for your ma, and I want you to see she doesn't have to."

When he put it to me like that, as bad as I wanted to go, I knew better than to argue. Two days later, old Sundown, fat and long-haired from his winter's rest, and Pa's packmule, loaded with supplies, stood ready to go. Pa kissed Ma good-bye, then turned to me and shook hands like I was a grown man. I knew by that he was expecting me to behave like one, and it made me real proud.

By the time another year was out, and we hadn't heard from him, Ma was wondering if she'd ever see Pa again. She was even considering selling the homestead to Milt Adams and going back to her folks in the East. Sure Pa wouldn't want that, I put my foot down.

"I ain't gonna let you do it," I told her. "Pa's coming home. I know he is."

"We can't make a living here," Ma argued. "There's too much for you and me to do, and we've imposed on the neighbors enough as it is."

"Well, we won't have to anymore," I said, "'cause I'm big enough now I can handle it. I'll work harder. You'll see."

Ma finally gave in for the time being, saying that we'd wait it out for another year and, after that, if Pa wasn't back, she was pulling out of this God-forsaken country.

Then one afternoon, when we'd given up all hope, he came riding in. I'd just finished putting up the first crop of hay and was fooling around with Callie's new-born calf. I heard hoofbeats and looked up to see who was coming. I couldn't believe my eyes. Old Sundown was moving down the trail a couple of hundred yards away. He was thin and ribby and so tired he could hardly move along. Something was draped over his back. I wasn't sure what it was for a minute or two, then I realized it was Pa. I went to hollering at the top of my voice, and Ma came running from the cabin.

"What is it, Sam?" she called.

"It's Pa! He's come home! And somethin's wrong!"

I got to Sundown first. When I grabbed his bridle reins, I could see Pa had tied himself to the saddle to keep from falling off, and he clung with his arms around the horse's neck. His left shoulder was crusted with blood, and a watery ooze bubbled from a wound in his back. I could see the stump of an arrow sticking out.

"Ma!" I yelled. "He's got an arrow in him!"

She was there by that time, and lifted Pa's face from where it rested against Sundown's shoulder. With trembling fingers, she pulled back his eyelid.

"Quick, Sam!" she said. "Help me get him in the house."

She untied him and we eased him to the ground. Pa was a big man, and though he was awful thin from his months on the trail, we had a hard time making it to the bedroom with him. We put him on the bed, and I pulled off his boots while Ma peeled away the blood-caked shirt from his wound. It looked mighty red and nasty, and Ma got a clean white cloth and wiped the dirt away. She cleaned the dust and grime from Pa's face and whiskers, and he slowly opened his eyes. He stared at her for a little while, I guess not sure where he was, then took hold of her hand.

"Mollie," he muttered.

She rubbed his forehead with her fingers, and the tears ran down her face. "Now lie quiet, John. We're goin' to take care of you."

"I . . . I thought . . . I'd never . . . make it," Pa mumbled. "Them damn . . . Kiawas . . ." His voice trailed off.

"Was it them that got Charlotte?" I wanted to know, thinking maybe he'd found her. But Pa couldn't answer me because he'd gone off again.

31

"Quick, Sam!" Ma ordered. "Get my bag."

I ran to the kitchen and got it from the shelf. When I came back, Pa was moaning like he was trying to come out of it again. He didn't open his eyes but started to mutter.

"Ain't . . . no use. Mollie . . . Two years I've searched . . . She must be—dead."

That old tortured look crossed Ma's face again as she worked with him, and I had to gulp to push the lump down in my throat. Pa went on trying to talk.

"Ain't no place . . . left to look. She's just— dead . . . !"

His voice trailed off again, and Ma reached for her black bag. She took out a sharp, thin-bladed knife and a roll of white bandage. I'll never forget how bitter she sounded when she said, "The dear Lord have mercy on me . . . but I hate them. I'll never forgive them for what they've done."

She went to the stove and held the knife over the live coals until it turned from bright red to white then came back to Pa's side. I watched her, not sure what she was going to do, and when she leaned over Pa and I saw that knife going toward his wound, I got sick to my stomach. I started to run for the door but Ma stopped me.

"Now don't be gittin' puny, Sam," she said. "I need your help, and can't be frettin' about you doin' somethin' foolish. Hand me them tweezers."

I swallowed hard, and tried to think about Charlotte to keep my mind off what Ma was doing while I handed her instruments. The sweat ran down her face and dripped on the front of her dress, but she kept right at it. When Pa cried out, I jumped like she'd touched me with that hot knife. Then Ma held up the head of an arrow.

"It's a miracle it didn't kill him, Sam," was all she said.

Hard as I tried, I couldn't help being sick, and I ran outside and hung over the porch rail until I vomited. Sometime later, I went back inside and sidled up to Pa's bed. He looked so pale and sick it scared the wadding out of me.

"Ma!" I blurted out. "He's dyin', ain't he?"

"Hush, Sam," she said. "Don't be sayin' such things."

"Shouldn't we pray for him?" I asked.

"What do you think I've been doin' all this time?" she answered. "Now you better take care of your pa's horse."

I found Sundown by the haystack, too tired to even eat. I took him to the corral and unsaddled him, thinking all the time I ought to say a prayer for Pa, too. Sometimes God seemed hard for me to talk to, but I figured it was because I only did it when I needed Him. All at once, I dropped to my knees.

"Pa's hurt bad, God," I said. "He sure needs your help to make it. Me and Ma have done all we can. Now it's up to you."

When I got to my feet, my throat felt full, and I had trouble keeping the tears back. But when I turned Sundown loose in the corral, something told me right then and there I didn't have to worry. Pa was sure going to get well.

Chapter Six

Later that evening, when I went into the cabin, I looked in on Pa. Ma had his shoulder bandaged, and he was sound asleep. By his deep breathing, I could tell he was resting well. Ma, completely give out, sat by his bed, her head in her arms. I watched her for a few minutes, then went back to the kitchen to write her a note.

"Please forgive me, Ma." I wrote, "I've got to know for sure about Charlotte."

I propped it up on the kitchen table and, putting some bacon and cornbread in a flour sack, I slipped out. I got Gray Back from the corral and put Pa's saddle on him. I made sure the headband was still hidden away in one of the saddlebags, and put Pa's rifle in the saddle scabbard. I rode out as quiet as I could, and when I reached the hill above the homestead, I stopped for one last look. The light still shone from the kitchen window, and for a minute, I wondered if I was doing the right thing. Then I remembered Ma's sad, tormented look, like there was nothing else to hope for, when Pa told her he was sure Charlotte was dead, and I pushed Gray Back on.

It didn't seem so far to the Old Smoky this time, and when we pulled up at the edge, Gray Back hadn't forgot his last bout with it, and he wasn't about to let it happen again. I cussed him and knocked him around, and we had it out pretty good. I guess he finally decided I had more stubborn than he did, and let me have my way. We got across easy enough this time, since Russian had showed me the best crossing.

When we pulled out on the other side, I watched for
Russian to come out of his cabin and B'ar Killer to
set up a holler. When nothing happened, I began to
worry for fear Russian had moved on to some other
place.

I stopped in front of his cabin and dismounted. I
tied Gray Back to a post and went to try the door.
It was locked. I looked around a bit then tried it
again. Disgusted, I kicked it with my boot heel and
headed back for my horse. I'd just put my foot in the
stirrup when I heard a loud moan coming from inside
of the cabin. I ran back to the door and shook it.

"Russian!" I yelled. "Are you in there?"

I about had the gizzard scared out of me when a
rifle blasted, and a bullet crashed through the door
above my head. I dropped to the ground and bellied
along the side of the cabin toward the window. The
moaning grew louder, and then all at once I recognized
Russian's drunken voice as he bellered out trying to
sing:

> "*I swallered a b'ar,*
> *Not far, over there.*
> *But I really didn't do it;*
> *I was drunk. T'was a skunk!*"

Then he whooped it up and howled at the top of
his voice like he'd really come up with something
great. I found an empty wooden barrel and rolled it
up to the window so I could peek inside. I couldn't
believe the way that cabin looked. It was in shambles,
with dirty broken dishes strewn all over the place. The
cot was turned upside down, and the bedding piled
in a heap in the corner. Russian sat propped up against
the overturned table, several empty whiskey jugs
around him, and a half-filled one in his lap. B'ar Killer

lay curled up beside him, and I'm not sure he hadn't had a load of booze himself. He had his head between his paws watching the old trapper like they were the only ones left in the world.

I struggled through the window and grabbed a half-filled bucket of water that sat on a bench nearby. That was the first B'ar Killer seemed to know I was around. He growled and the hair raised up on the back of his neck a bit before he recognized me. Then his tail went to slapping on the floor to welcome me. I dumped the bucket of water down over Russian's head.

"You dirty old drunken trapper!" I yelled. "Maybe this'll sober you up!"

Russian coughed and sputtered then looked up at me with bleary eyes.

"Huh . . . *huh?* . . . Who are you?" He growled drunkenly. "I ain't never seen you before in my life. Tear 'is leg off. Killer!"

B'ar Killer must not have heard him right, for he got up and came over, trying to lick my face. I shoved him down, disgusted clear through with them both.

"Nobudy ever listens to me," complained Russian.

"You can't blame 'em," I told him. "You're nothin' but an ol' drunk! Even your dog ain't got no respect for you. You oughta be ashamed . . . and if you ain't, I am!"

I was so full of mad, I unlocked the door and slammed out of the cabin. I went to Gray Back and leaned against her for a bit trying to make up my mind what to do now. I had to have Russian's help. I knew he could speak nearly every tongue in the Indian territory; at least that's what he said, and I figured if anyone could help me find Charlotte, it would be him. Finally, I turned back into the cabin.

"Come on!" I said, jerking him a good one. "You're goin' with me!"

"Huh? What's that?" He rolled his eyes back in his head. "What are ya talkin' about?"

"You're goin' with me to find my sister, that's what!"

"You're crazy!" he bellered, grabbing his head with both hands. "I ain't goin' nowhere, not with a smart-aleck kid like you! Sic 'im, Killer!"

B'ar Killer whined and padded over to Russian and licked his face. I tried to drag the trapper to his feet.

"Drunk or not, I need someone who knows Injun country, and you're comin' with me," I said, trying to sound tough.

Russian gave me a shove. "Leave me be, you fool kid! I got my trappin' to do."

"I'll bet you ain't trapped in more'n a year," I said. I flashed the gold headband in front of him. "And besides, I'm willin' ta pay you right handsome. You can have all the gold we find once you take me to them Injuns that stole my sister."

Russian laughed so loud the window panes rattled, then he eyed the headband. "You blame ninny! Your sister's long been scalped and hangin' in a tree!"

I got mad clear through. I grabbed him and shook him the best I could. "I'll take my chances on that. Now come on! We're headin' out!"

He jabbed me in the stomach and sent me flying across the room. I crashed against the up-ended cot, the breath mostly knocked out of me. What was left came out in slow, sharp grunts.

"I mean what I say . . . when I say it!" bellered Russian. "Ain't no brat tellin' me what to do. Ain't thet right, Killer?"

37

B'ar Killer trotted over to me and jumped on me with his front feet, licking my face good. I shoved him off. And having gotten most of my breath back by this time, I got to my feet and glared at Russian. I wasn't ready to give up yet.

"You're comin' with me!" I shouted at him, "even if it means stayin' here and tormentin' you 'til you do, So jest make up your mind to that!"

I went to the fireplace and threw some wood on the coals. Russian glared at me, then started to laugh. I ignored him and went about fixing us something to eat.

Later, after I'd gotten some food down him and he'd sobered up a bit, I sat by the fire, flashing my headband in its light. I stared at Russian where he lay on his cot across the room. He suddenly seemed to be hypnotized by the gold, as I turned the band in my hands. All at once, he jerked to a sitting position.

"Will you stop your starin'!" he yelled out. "Or do I have to cut your throat?"

I ignored him and went on flashing the headband.

"You can bet there's plenty more gold where this come from," I said, like I was just talking to myself. "Prob'bly stacks and stacks of it."

"You ain't temptin' me with thet," said Russian. "If I want to go, I will, and if I don't, I won't. And that's it!"

I could tell I had him coming around, and I kept rolling the headband over and over in my hands. From the corner of my eye, I could see his greedy look, and I figured if I knew anything about this old trapper, come morning, we'd both be riding out of here together to look for my sister.

Chapter Seven

The next morning, I watched Russian as he tied a bunch of whiskey jugs on his packmule, grumbling all the time he was doing it.

"I wouldn't be goin' a step with you, you ornery young pup, if you didn't make me think of my own dead kid." He stepped back to look at his mule. "Now ain't that a pretty sight?"

"I don't see why you need all that stuff," I told him, meaning the whiskey.

"I never travel without it," he said. "Yessir, everythin' thet's near and dear to me's strapped on thet mule . . . 'ceptin' maybe B'ar Killer."

Hearing his name, B'ar Killer trotted to the trapper's side and looked up at him, whining and wagging his tail. Russian paid him no attention as he struggled up on his big gelding, and we were soon moving up the narrow trail that led out of the clearing.

I was sure happy to be on our way. In spite of what Pa and Russian said, I was certain Charlotte was still alive and, come rain or shine, I didn't figure on turning back until I found her.

There was no hurrying Russian, and he took his time going through mountains, and heavy wooded country, and even the flat lands. He stopped often to take a slug or two of booze. Every time I looked at the skyline, it seemed farther away. I hadn't realized the world could be so big.

It took the most part of two days to cross what I figured was close to fifty miles of desert. The white crust of clay and sand finally moved up into rolling hills and scrub oak. We climbed into high country and twisted pines, and Russian shot a white-tailed antelope for camp meat.

In the early evening of the third day, we slid off our horses in front of Diar Crow's Trading Post. It made me think of a fat, ugly horned toad squatting on a rock in the sun. It was resting on the south shore of White Horse Lake, with high red cliffs behind, looking like they were put there just on purpose to guard it. The place seemed alive with Indians. And traders with long beards and dirty buckskins stood among them. Most of them paid us no nevermind, but others looked at us like they thought we were up to no good. They jabbered to one another, waving their hands in sign language, but I couldn't understand a thing they said. Then a tall, rawboned feller came striding from among a bunch of Indians toward us. His beard was full of dried tobacco juice, like it hadn't been cleaned for six Easter Sundays, and his hair hadn't had a comb in it for about as long. He seemed friendly enough, though, the way he came right up to Russian and shook hands with him.

"Wal, if it ain't Russian Habbakuk!" he boomed out. "What brings you here?"

"I've teamed up with a new pardner, Diar," said Russian, "and we gotta little searchin' to do. Shake hands with Sam Sutter, the fiestiest kid I've ever come up against."

When Diar Crow shook hands with me, I felt my knuckles snap. I thought they were broke and almost yelled out, but gritted my teeth and stood it.

"I'm glad to know you, Sam," he said, then turned back to Russian. "You're stayin' for supper and spendin' the night, ain't ya?"

"You shore can bet on thet, Diar," said Russian.

"We been a long time comin', and a good meal'll taste mighty good."

We unsaddled our horses and unpacked the mule, then hobbled them in the grass along the shore of the lake. Russian ordered B'ar Killer to stay with the gear.

Later, Diar fed us a good supper of venison and wild onions and dried corn he'd traded for with the Indians. I ate 'til I thought my eyeballs would pop out of my head, but that wouldn't make a dent in what Russian put away.

I was nervous about being around the bunch of rough-looking traders, but there was one ugly half-breed that made the air raise on the back of my neck every time he looked at me. I stayed close as I could to Russian 'til he sent me out to fetch the gold headband from my saddlebag. Russian showed it around.

"We're lookin' for this boy's sister, who was stole by some Injuns that dropped this," he said. "Have you seen any redskins with anythin' like it?"

Diar and some of the others came over to examine it.

"It's shore strange ta me," said Diar.

The others shook their heads, and Russian handed it back to me. About that time, I felt someone breathing down my neck. I almost jumped out of my skin as I turned to see the half-breed, the evil in his eyes showing through as he stared at the headband. Russian opened his mouth in a yawn that could swaller a beaver.

"Well, I best be gittin' this runt to bed," he said, then patted his stomach. "Food shore was good, Diar."

I was glad to get out of the trading post just to get away from that half-breed's stare. In just a minute, Diar follered us. When we got a little way from the post, he said, "I wouldn't let thet gold trinket be layin' around careless like, Habbakuk . . . not with that breed here. I'd sleep with one eye open and my gun handy. If you don't, come mornin' you might both be minus your scalps."

I shuddered, and I'll bet my eyes bunged out some, but Russian just stretched his arms over his head and yawned like he wasn't in the least concerned. We heard B'ar Killer growl and looked toward him. He was bristling at the half-breed, who had just stepped out of the trading post and was heading his way.

"B'ar Killer don't care much for breeds," chuckled Russian, starting for our gear.

The half-breed switched direction when he saw us, and B'ar Killer kept on growling until he was out of sight.

We wrapped ourselves in our blankets, and Russian took a long drink from his jug, then, grunting, turned over and went to snoring. I heard old B'ar Killer sniff a time or two from his place between us and felt pretty safe with him there. I couldn't help thinking about that half-breed, though, and had a hard time going to sleep. So I went to counting stars. I got to wondering about Ma and Pa, if they were all right, and for the first time, I felt a little homesick.

The next morning we were up early and had breakfast over and the horses saddled before anyone else was stirring at the trading post. Russian waited long enough to get some more booze from Diar, and we moved out on the trail. We took the first one that led off toward the purple-ridged mountains to the east of us. Russian, riding ahead and leading the packmule, and with his rifle handy, kept stopping to look toward the wooded thickets and rocks that edged the trail. I knew he was nervous about something, and seeing him that way made me uneasy, too. All at once, B'ar Killer growled deep in his throat, and Russian's rifle went to his shoulder. I heard another shot as he fired, and I felt something tug at the sleeve of my jacket. I grabbed my left arm, thinking I was shot for sure. Then I got a glimpse of what Russian was after, as a brown blotch disappeared in the gray-green brush. Russian's gun spit another cloud of smoke. After a third shot he grunted and put his rifle back in the saddle scabbard.

"That ought ta take care of 'im," he said, turning to me. "Did you get hit?"

Gulping, I held up my arm to show him the jagged bullet hole in my sleeve.

"It—it was c-c-close," I stammered.

Russian gazed at it a bit then chuckled. "Let that be a lesson to you, runt. Don't ever go to sleep when you're out in this country. Instead of your sleeve, you might lose your scalp."

"Who—who was it?" I asked, still so full of scare my teeth chattered.

"That half-breed Diar warned us about . . . but it was no more'n I expected, and I was ready for 'im. A life don't mean a thing to fellers like him if you've got somethin' they want."

"You mean my gold headband? Do you think he'll try it again?"

"He'll have to do some patchin' on 'imself first. I think I nicked 'im in the shoulder my last shot, but I ain't waitin' around to find out."

We got out of there in a hurry, and I noticed Russian never relaxed until we were out in the open country again.

Chapter Eight

After leaving the trading post, our search for Charlotte took us from one territory into another. We questioned so many trappers and Indians I lost all track of time and distance. I could tell it was wearing on Russian, and wondered how much longer the cranky old feller was going to stick it out. I got my answer one night as we camped at a place Russian called Shadow Springs. I brought him a pot of coffee I'd just made for him out of the goodness of my heart.

"Durned if you don't make the worst coffee!" he yelled, spewing a mouthful out on the ground.

"I told you I never made it before," I said. "We don't drink—"

He didn't let me finish, but grabbed the pot and dumped it into the fire, grumbling, "Even worse than my dead squaw's!"

When he talked about her, I usually knew enough to keep my mouth shut. Puffing and grunting, he went about making another pot of coffee. I let him get it on the fire before I got the courage to mention something that had been bothering me for some time.

"Russian," I said, "did ya really have a son?"

He gave me a sharp look. "I told ya, didn't I?"

"Did you—did you really—slit his throat?"

He roared laughing, and what he said next made my eyes bulge. "Course I did! What do you think I made that stew out of?" Then all of a sudden he got real serious and had a faraway look in his eyes.

"He was a good boy. And like I told you before, he put me in mind of you. His mother was Cheyenne, one of the finest lil' women you'd ever meet. Bought 'er off ol' Shokabob for two jugs of booze. Damn pox got 'em both."

He didn't say anymore, but just sat staring into the fire with a sad look, like he hurt down deep. It was the first time I'd seen him like that, and it made me uneasy. Thinking I could get his mind off what troubled him, I said, "You'd think after this time, we'd find some clues about Charlotte. It's like searchin' for ghosts, ain't it?"

"You cain't expect folks to know somethin' about a tribe thet don't exist," he grumbled. "Every day it gits more clear that you brought me on a wild goose chase. You might as well know, I don't aim to go on."

"Russian, you ain't quittin'?"

"Fact is, I've a mind to head back first thing in the mornin'."

"But you can't!"

"Cain't I, now? And jest what's stoppin' me?"

"But I've gotta have you along. How else will I talk to them Injuns? They'll scalp me for sure."

"Then won't your ma and pa have a good reason to grieve, . . . both of their kids hangin' in a tree?"

I got to my feet so mad I wanted to hit him with a rock.

"Well, I don't care if you do go back!" I yelled. "I'm goin' on 'til I find Charlotte, and you can be sure when I do find that gold, you ain't gettin' one little piece of it, you ol' fat yeller belly!"

"Why you lil' . . ." Russian sputtered, leaping to his feet, and I got ready to take off, sure as the devil he was going to whale the tar out of me. Then he calmed right down. "Oh, what's the use . . . ! You're too thick-skulled to listen to reason. Your pa spends two years searchin', and we're been out here nigh on to a month now, and you still think you're goin' to find somethin' jest around the next tree. . . . All right then. We're three days from the Cheyennes, and after thet I'm headin' back, and you can go to hell for all I care!"

He went to pour himself a cup of coffee, still grumbling to himself about "havin' to traipse all over the country with a dumb, senseless kid."

Three days later, we rode into the Cheyenne camp. I'd be telling a whopper if I said I wasn't scared. The women and kids gawked at us like we were a couple of freaks. A bunch of mongrel dogs set up a holler and came at B'ar Killer like they were going to tear him apart. I expected to see a dog-pile, but he just snarled at them a time or two and kept right on follering us. Russian went on like he hobnobbed every day with the Cheyennes, and even old B'ar Killer acted right at home from then on.

We passed by a squaw with a basket on her head. Russian stopped his horse, and I pulled up beside him.

"Now, ain't she a purty lil' thing?" he said. "Wonder how old Shokabob'd like to swap 'er for a smart-aleck white kid!"

This spooked me like nothing else he'd ever said. I guess I was thinking back the way he looked when he talked about buying his wife for some booze. Then he roared, laughing, and I knew he was just having some fun with me.

The Indian woman gazed at us in a strange way, then sidled over where several others pounded corn on a big flat rock. They all stopped their work to watch us. Then I noticed an old Indian brave sitting among them. His clothes were tattered, and he had more wrinkles in his face than a crumpled piece of brown paper. His long, gray hair hung down his back and was tied with a rawhide thong. His eyes were so weak and watery, I don't know how he could see what he was doing.

Russian kicked his horse and I follered. A bunch of warriors gathered behind us and, plenty nervous, I pushed up close to Russian. He kept on riding, not bothering to look back until he pulled up in front of the biggest teepee in the camp. As we got off our horses, a tall, older Indian brave stepped from the tent's opening. By the way he was dressed, I was sure he had to be Shokabob. He wore a headband of bright feathers, and beads covered his fringed jacket and buckskin pants. His hair hung in long braids in front of his shoulders, and I thought he sure made a handsome chief. Russian didn't say a word but just took a jug from his packmule and handed it to Shokabob. The chief took a big drink and licked his lips. Russian told him in Cheyenne why we were there, and I took the headband from my saddle bag, holding it so the chief could see it. He took it from me and looked at it close. He shook his head, and as he handed it back, he said something to Russian.

"What'd he say, Russian?" I asked, all excited.

"Jist like I figured . . . he don't know nothin,' either."

I felt as let down as a wooden bucket dropped in a dry well. The Cheyennes had been my last hope. Shokabob jabbered something to Russian and kept pointing to his tent. Russian grinned and turned to me.

"Now," he said, "if you'll excuse me, Sam Isaac, I've been invited to a lil' social gatherin', follerin' which, I'm headin' back."

I was so disappointed I couldn't say a word, and

just stood there with my head down while they went inside the tent. When I looked up, I was completely surrounded by Indians. They all were staring at the gold band, and I put it on my head so they could get a better look. They moved into a tight circle, really giving it the once-over. All of a sudden, I jumped like a lizard on a hot skillet as an eerie screech came from behind me.

"OOOeeeaaahhh!"

I whirled around. The old Indian I'd seen pounding corn with the women earlier was staring at the band on my head, his watery eyes wide and his mouth hanging open. His fingers reached for it like eagle claws, and I ducked back out of his way. He still came on, making strange noises that didn't even sound human. He made a grab for the band, and I dodged out of his reach again. He stretched out his arms, whimpering, like he was pleading for me to let him have it.

Russian's voice came from behind me. "Let 'im have it, boy. He ain't gonna lift your scalp."

I turned around. Russian and Shokabob had come from the teepee and were standing together watching. I took the headband off and handed it to the old Indian. He rubbed his fingers across it like it was something special to him. Tears came to his eyes and ran down his cheeks. He kept whimpering and making strange noises, and I turned to Russian.

"What's he doin'? Does he know somethin'?"

Russian spoke to Shokabob in Cheyenne, and Shokabob replied.

"What's the matter with him, Russian? Why don't he talk?" I asked.

"Poor old fool," he explained, ". . . Came here years ago with his tongue cut out, in the dead of winter, and tried to steal a scrap of food. These

48

lovin' Cheyennes took 'im in and condemned him to a squaw's work fer the rest of 'is life."

"Maybe he's—"

Russian cut me off. "They call 'im Cut Tongue, but don't know who he is or where 'e's from. So don't be gittin' your hopes up, boy."

Shokabob spoke real harsh to the old Indian and motioned us to foller him into the tent. Cut Tongue hobbled along behind, still hanging on to my headband. Inside, Shokabob sat on his blankets and gestured for us to sit near him. Then he began asking the old man questions in Cheyenne. Cut Tongue answered him in weak sign language, all the time rolling his watery eyes, trying to make us understand. I could tell Russian couldn't even make out what he said. Cut Tongue held up the gold band, pointing to the markings on it, then, with his finger, slowly drew something on the dirt floor. Shokabob's eyes lit up, and he brokenly gave the translation. Russian repeated it to me so I could understand.

"The engravings mean something," he said. "Something about a great struggle . . . a struggle at Crooked Sky . . . to be able to wear ancient gold."

I gazed at Russian, then at Cut Tongue, who now had the band on the floor in front of him. He bent over it, crying and moaning in a pitiful way.

"What's wrong with him?" I asked Russian.

Shokabob mumbled something to Russian, and I could see the old trapper was beginning to catch on.

"The old codger claims the gold band belongs to him," he said. "Says he earned it at Crooked Sky by passing some sorta great test of courage!"

"Crooked Sky!" I gasped, all excited now. "That's what we've been lookin' for, Russian. That's gotta be where Charlotte is!"

"I ain't never heerd of such a place," he said,

49

"an' I ain't goin' lookin' fer a place I've never heerd of."

"Well, ask him!" I insisted. "Ask him where it is!"

Russian spoke to Shokabob again, and the chief talked a bit to Cut Tongue. The old Indian looked first at Russian, then at me. He started to wave his hands and make strange noises.

"He says he won't tell us where it is, but he'll show us," said Russian. "Sounds like he wants to die with 'is own people."

"Tell him we'll take him there, if that's what he wants," I cried, ". . . and he can have the headband, too. Tell him, Russian!"

Russian glared at me. "Are you plumb loco? He can barely teeter around camp. He'd last about one day on the trail. Besides, I already told you where I'm goin'."

"But that was if we didn't find any clues here. And now we know where Charlotte is!" I was beginning to feel desperate. "Please, Russian, ya gotta help me! Let's pack up and get goin'!"

"No!" he yelled, and I didn't like the way he was looking at me. "You heard what I said . . . and this time I mean it!"

Chapter Nine

I guess I'll never know what made Russian change his mind, but the next morning when I got up he was already saddled and packed ready to go. Cut Tongue was putting a few things on a paint Indian pony, and I looked at Russian thinking maybe he'd explain things to me. He wouldn't look my way even, but grumbled, "Durn fool me! Listenin' to a brat!"

I grinned to myself, knowing if I was smart I'd just keep my mouth shut. It didn't take me long to put my gear together and get mounted up. We rode out of the Cheyenne camp with Russian in the lead, followed by Cut Tongue, then me and the packmule. B'ar Killer brought up the rear. The whole tribe was there to see us off. Russian took one last swig from his half-empty jug of booze, then tossed it to Shokabob. The chief caught it, grinning from ear to ear, and raised his hand in friendship to the old trapper. I understood then how Russian kept on such good terms with the Indians.

It seemed we follered old Cut Tongue's directions for weeks. We traveled through all kinds of country, from long stretches of desert to mountain slopes thick with timber. Russian stopped often to question Cut Tongue, and the old Indian lifted a shaky hand and motioned him on to the far horizon. Russian finally made him take the lead, and he kept behind, drinking more often from his jug of booze. I got so tired, I thought I couldn't stay in the saddle any longer.

"I shoulda never come," complained Russian. "You ol' coot! Whar ya takin' us?"

If Cut Tongue heard him, he paid no never-mind and kept right on going, winding through big rocks and scrub junipers. Later, I noticed Cut Tongue acting uneasy, looking every which way and squinting off into the rocks. All at once he stopped, and we pulled up behind him.

"What's wrong?" I asked Russian.

"We're in Apache country, and the ol' buzzard knows it," he said.

That scared me, and the roots of my hair started to prickle. I'd heard for years about the Apaches and how fierce they were. Everything was so quiet, I could almost hear the rocks whispering. I breathed a sigh of relief when Cut Tongue finally gave us the signal to move on.

It was a couple of hours later we entered a small clearing. There were some pockets in the rocks filled with water from a recent rain, and we could camp and give our horses a good drink.

"This is where we stop," said Russian as he got down and took his rifle from his saddle. "You water and care for the horses, Sam, then set up camp while I do a little scoutin'."

I got off my horse, and Russian pulled my rifle from its scabbard and handed it to me.

"And you'd be wise to keep this handy and your eyes peeled," he added.

He disappeared in the rocks follered by B'ar Killer. Cut Tongue got down and handed me his horse's reins, then taking his tattered blanket, he went to lie down under a ledge of overhanging rock. As he got back in well out of sight, I noticed how his eyes shifted here and there. I watched him for a minute, then watered the horses and turned them loose. The sun was almost down, and I went to the edge of the clearing, hoping for some sight of Russian. When I didn't see him, I suddenly got fidgety.

"I wish that old trapper would get back here," I muttered.

All at once, a fierce scream pierced the air and I jumped so hard I almost left my skin hanging on a bush. I whirled around, whipping my knife out. Then I saw an eagle diving toward the ground, his wings tight against his side. He was coming so fast I didn't see how he could stop before he splattered on the rocks. But it didn't happen that way at all. He hit something, all right, but it was a little ground squirrel that thought he was hid out in the bushes. There was a lot of thrashing around, and then I heard a whimpering cry that sent me dashing over to give the squirrel a hand. I was too late, and the old eagle took off and soared upward, the squirrel still whimpering and struggling in his claws. Feeling sick about that little helpless animal, I put my knife back in my belt and headed toward the horses.

I heard a whispering sound behind me. Before I could turn around, a hand clamped over my mouth, and my arms were pinned to my side. I almost died right there when the ugly face of that half-breed from Diar Crow's leered down at me. In a flash, he jerked the headband loose from my belt, and when I saw his hand come up with a knife in it, I was too full of scare to even yell. He reach for my hair, and I lashed out with my feet, kicking at him and trying to twist away.

About that time, from somewhere in the rocks, a hairy shape came diving into the fight. It was old B'ar Killer, roaring like a grizzly, and the weight of his heavy body knocked us both to the ground. It broke the half-breed's hold on me, and I rolled clear.

I scrambled to my feet and let B'ar Killer have at him. He kept him on the ground, mauling him good.

"Russian!" I yelled, then turned to run for my gun where I'd leaned it up against a rock. I didn't make it. Right in front of me stepped the meanest-looking Apache I'd ever seen. He grabbed me, and I screeched like he was already lifting my scalp. Cut Tongue raised up behind him, and the old Indian got hold of his arm and hung on with all he had. Still keeping his grip on me, the Apache slung the near-helpless old man to the ground.

I thought I was sure a goner. Then I saw Russian diving through the air like that eagle. He flattened the Apache and sent him sprawling. I was thrown free, and before the brave could get up, Russian was upon him.

I got to my feet and took a quick look around. Cut Tongue was disappearing in the rocks. B'ar Killer and the breed were having an awful battle. B'ar Killer had ripped the flesh on the man's arm with his sharp fangs. And howling with pain, the breed tried again and again to sink the knife into B'ar Killer's body.

"Russian! Your dog!" I hollered, glancing at Russian and the Apache. They were both on their feet, crouching as they each sparred to get in the first lick. The trapper, using his rifle as a club, made a swing at the Indian's head just as I yelled, distracting him. He missed, hitting the brave a glancing blow on the shoulder. The Indian hunched forward, grabbing his arm and his face twisting in pain. Russian whirled and headed for B'ar Killer. The breed, bleeding something awful from B'ar Killer's fangs, was straddle of him, and the dog made feeble attempts to get to him. At that moment, the Apache tackled Russian from behind and dragged him to the ground. I gave B'ar Killer a quick look and saw the breed raise his knife high to finish him off. I threw my rifle to my shoulder and fired, just as he drove it into the dog's body. He threw his hands in the air, his body falling backward on the ground, and I knew I had killed a man for the first time.

A little sick, I turned to see how Russian was making out. He and the Apache were on the ground having a mighty struggle. I threw another bullet into the chamber of my rifle and tried to get the Indian lined up in my sights. They twisted and turned every which way, and I couldn't get a shot at the Apache without hitting Russian. I finally threw my rifle down and went in close to them. Russian's hard breathing let me know he was getting pretty tired. The Indian got on top of him and locked his legs around Russian's body. When his hand raised and I saw the glint of a knife, I dove at him, grabbing his hair. I jerked back, and the blade glanced off of the trapper's arm. He bellered like a mad bull, and I saw the blood spurt. I swear he rustled up more strength than six spans of mules going up a hill and twisted from under the Apache. He got ahold of the arm that held the knife and wrenched it so hard the Indian screeched in pain. I could see why when I heard the bone snap and the knife fall to the ground. Russian was on it like a cat on a bird, and before I more than had time to get out of the way, it quivered between the brave's shoulder like a fluttering hawk. He was out of the fight for good.

By the time we got to B'ar Killer's side, he already had a pool of blood beneath him. He whined faintly to Russian, and when the trapper went down on his knees, the dog raised his head and licked his hand. Russian's face was one of grief, rage and vengeance, like he didn't know which to show first.

"Them dirty Apache polecats!" he raged. "Killin' my dog!"

His face twisted in fury, and his voice became soft and raspy as he choked out his hurt.

"There'll be some . . . black hair hangin' . . . from my belt to pay fer this deed," he whispered, the tears running down his face. "He's—he's all I had."

I kneeled down at his side, wanting to give him comfort, but the only thing that seemed right was to stroke B'ar Killer's head.

"He saved my life," I said. "Two times he saved it."

Russian slowly nodded. The dog raised his head and licked his hand again. Russian bent over him, and I could see he was having a hard time of it. Then B'ar Killer gave a little gasp, and the life went out of him. I couldn't take anymore, and jumped up and ran over to lay my head against a rock. In a few minutes, I looked back at Russian. He was still bent over his dog, and I knew he must feel as bad about him as I did Charlotte.

I raised my eyes to see Cut Tongue coming out of hiding. Without a sound, he gazed at the awful sight around him. Then I remembered my headband and went over to the half-breed I had killed. It lay in the rocks a short distance from where he had fallen, and I bent to pick it up. I stared at it, then the breed, and shuddered. I wondered if he ever figured, as he sneaked around the country waiting for a chance to steal my headband, that it would cost him his life.

Chapter Ten

It was twilight, and a light rain was falling when me and Russian stood by B'ar Killer's grave. The old trapper looked so sorrowful, I could hardly bear to watch him. He kneeled to put a cross made of two sticks at one end of the mound.

"Maybe I shouldn'ta took time to plant 'im," he said, his voice shaking, "but it's—it's like partin' with my own kin."

I put my hand on his shoulder, thinking maybe I could comfort him a little, but he sort of shrugged it off and got to his feet.

"We'd better be gittin' outa here," he said.

I got the horses and mule and helped old Cut Tongue up on his pony. By the time we pulled out of camp, the rain was pelting down on us good and hard. Lightning flashed, and thunder coughed and roared across the mountains. The night was so black I had a hard time keeping Russian in sight. The only way I was sure he was ahead of me was by his horse's hoofbeats and the little glimpses I'd get of him in the lightning flashes.

Soaked to the skin, we must have gone on like this for two hours before Russian finally pulled up in front of a small overhanging ledge. The thunder and lightning had stopped, but the rain had bellied down into a steady drizzle.

"It ain't the best shelter in the world," he said, getting off his horse, "but it sure as hell beats ridin' in this."

We unpacked the mule and I hobbled our horses

close by, while Russian built a fire in front of the ledge. He examined the blood-caked wound in his arm, then took a piece of dirty shirt from his saddle-bag to bind it up. The three of us were crowded in that little cave like three chickens in an egg. Russian's temper was short, and he grumbled a lot, but I paid no attention. I was so tired, I could have slept in a hog waller. I rolled up in a ball with my head on my wet coat, the smoke from the fire blowing over me. I'd have been asleep in another second, but all at once Russian yelled so loud I thought an Indian was lifting his scalp. I reared up expecting the worst, but in the firelight I could see he was having a time bandaging his arm. He tore into me like it was all my fault.

"If this don't do me in!" he raged, "I'll likely die of blood poisonin'! Should never a' let a young whelp like you talk me into this . . . traipsin' all over the country, nigh gittin' my throat slit . . . an' losin'— my dog . . . !"

I looked at him for a moment but didn't say anything. I went to helping him with his bandage.

"My mind's made up!" he ranted on. "I ain't goin' another step!"

When he came up with that again, I started boiling inside, but I had sense enough to keep still until he finished with the bandaging and cooled off a little.

Finally I said, "Then I reckon we'll just have to go on alone."

Russian gave me one of his favorite looks and snorted, "You and thet old coot? Why he don't even know where he's goin'."

"I came to find my sister," I said, "and I ain't givin' up now. Besides, we promised to take him back to his people, and that's what I aim to do!"

Russian snorted. "Ha! You'll both be dead in a week, I guarantee."

"We'll make it," I said. "God didn't help us to come this far just to let us die."

"God!" he bellered out. "Don't give no thanks to *Him!* It was me that brung you . . . not God! And it shore wasn't Him that saved you today!"

I scowled and turned my face away. When Russian got his mind set in a certain direction, there was no need of me trying to argue him out of it.

"Well, do as you durn please," he grumbled. "I don't have the will to fight you no more."

I lay back down on my coat and put the crook of my arm over my eyes like I was shutting out the firelight. Mostly, I didn't want Russian to catch me crying. I had good reason to bawl. It wasn't easy to go through what we had up until now, then give up. What I felt then wasn't just disappointment but downright despair.

When dawn came, the rain had stopped. I got up, hoping that Russian had changed his mind. We ate a quick breakfast without building a fire. And when he started separating the supplies, I knew he still intended to go back. There was enough water standing in puddles from the rain to give our horses a good drink, then Russian began tying his things behind his saddle. Me and Cut Tongue were already mounted, and I held the packmule's lead rope. I was sure put out at Russian, and feeling darn sorry for myself. The more I thought about it, the more my sorry turned to mad. No matter what, I was going on, but I didn't know what I was going to do without the old trapper. He took a long drink of booze from his bottle, then turned to see me glaring at him.

"Well!" he snapped. "What are ya gawkin' at?

You've got my mule, and now you shore ain't gonna git my horse so git goin'!"

He took another pull at his jug, draining it, then threw it on the ground.

"You shouldn't have no trouble findin' your way back," I said. "Just foller your empty jugs!"

Before he could say anything back, I whirled my horse and headed up the trail, motioning for Cut Tongue to fall in behind the packmule. When we had climbed a piece, I took a look back over my shoulder at Russian. He was gazing after us, a look of exasperation on his face, then got on his horse and headed back down the canyon.

We climbed up into the canyon, and I stopped to look down at the hills below us. Beyond them, the desert shimmered in the sun. There was no sign of Russian. We moved on, traveling along a little-used trail through the roughest country I'd ever been in. Shale and rock slipped away from the mountain, making long, loose slopes that we could barely creep along. The hot sun glared down on us, and I looked up to see what time it was. It was almost noon. I studied the mountains ahead for landmarks I'd be sure to remember, then hitched in my saddle to look back the way we'd come. I knew I had to depend on myself, now, to find my way back home when I found Charlotte.

Suddenly, my horse shied as a rattlesnake whirred its warning. With the britches near scared off me, I gouged my heels in Gray Back's ribs and got a quick glimpse of it coiled in a bush by the side of the trail. At the same time my horse snorted and lunged forward, the packmule jerked back, breaking loose and bolting back down the way we'd come. He slammed into Cut Tongue's pony, knocking him off-balance. The loose shale and rock started to slip as the horse tried to get his feet under him. He wallered and pitched with old Cut Tongue hanging on with all he had. All at once, the old Indian sailed into the rocks in a heap, his body jerking like he was having a looney fit, while his horse rolled on down the hill.

In the middle of it all, my horse started caving around like he thought he ought to be taking part. I finally got him quieted down before he got us in the same predicament, then got off to see what I could do for Cut Tongue. His face and hands were bleeding, and by his twisted body I knew he was hurt bad. He groaned in pain as I kneeled beside him, rolling his eyes back in his head and gasping, as though every breath would be his last. His horse was now on his feet, scared to move for fear he'd go rolling down the hill again. The packmule had stopped and was nibbling on a bush at the side of the trail. I went for Cut Tongue's pony and eased him back up beside the old Indian.

"Cut Tongue . . . you've got to try to get up," I said, tugging at him. "I can't get you back on your horse alone."

His answer was a loud groan.

"Please," I begged. "You've got to."

With my arm under his shoulders, I tried to lift him to a sitting position. He wailed so loud I almost dropped him.

"Come on, Cut Tongue," I pleaded. "Help me . . . please!"

At that moment, his eyes closed and his mouth sagged open. His body went limp and I eased him back on the rocks. I got to my feet so full of panic I didn't know what to do next. Here I was, left alone in this wild country with a bad hurt, or maybe even dead Indian on my hands, and no one to guide me to Charlotte. There was no way, either, I could keep my promise to get Cut Tongue back to his people. I went to beating the air with my fists and yelling like a wild man.

"I hate that Russian! I hate him . . . hate him . . . *hate him!*"

I heard my words echoing and bouncing off the ridges.

"Are you speakin' about me, runt?" Russian's voice came from behind me, then he roared, laughing.

I jerked around. He sat on his horse grinning at me, the packmule's lead rope and a whiskey jug in his hand.

Chapter Eleven

I wish I had old Russian's know-how. It wasn't long before he had a travois made and Cut Tongue on it. I'd never seen anything like it before, but Russian said the Indians used it all the time. It was a narrow bed made of small poles tied together on two long shafts that went up each side of Cut Tongue's pony. These were fastened to a rope that he looped around the horse's shoulders, so it would pull across his chest and drag the bed behind. Russian bent down and took a close look at Cut Tongue.

"Is he goin' to live?" I asked him.

"A while, I'd say," he replied. "Likely jest long enough ta git us good and lost in the desert. I shore as the devil hope he knows where he's takin' us."

Before I knew it, we were on our way again. I didn't keep track of the days we traveled, but I know we sure covered a lot of country. Every night when we stopped to camp, I expected Cut Tongue to be dead, but somehow the old Indian hung on with still enough strength to let us know we were headed in the right direction. We forced as much food and water down him as we could, and I guess his hope of getting back to his people was all that gave him the will to live.

The hot sun beat down on us until we were burned as crisp as a piece of bacon. Russian got crankier with every mile, and complained and grumbled until I wondered how long I could put up with it. Our water was getting low, and as we got deeper into the desert, I could see Russian was beginning to get uneasy. Cut Tongue directed us to a water hole, and when we got there, it was nothing but a soupy, curdled pool of mud. Russian cursed the old Indian, then turned on me.

"I wish I'd never laid eyes on you," he growled. "You ain't brought me nothin' but misery."

I had to bite my tongue to keep from yelling back at him, and I was glad I did because I could see we had something else to worry about. Russian saw it almost as soon as I did, and his eyes narrowed as he watched the thick, yellow cloud rolling along the floor of the desert toward us. It lifted higher until the sky was all gray, and the sun became a big red ball. Then with sort of a whispering sound, the sand came, pricking our skin like a million cactus thorns. It was like the sky and the wind was helping the desert to turn us back.

We pushed our horses together, side by side, so as not to lose each other, and to get what protection we could from them. It was some time before the storm blew itself out, and the air cleared. Cut Tongue's travois was almost buried in the sand. Russian dug him out and gave him a swaller or two of water, and we were on our way again.

It was late afternoon when Russian pulled up and and got off to take the last waterbag from the packmule. It was empty. Somehow, a small hole had rubbed in the bag, and the water had all leaked out. Russian slammed it on the ground and stomped on it. He tilted his last whiskey jug, and it was empty, too. Cursing, he threw it down and went to glaring at me.

"What do we do now?" he barked. "No water, no booze!"

I squinted off into the hills, ignoring him the best

64

I could. Then I saw something that made me sit up and take notice. It wasn't very clear through the heat waves, but it sure looked to me like a big wall of rock that went on forever. It would disappear, then come back again. I didn't say anything to Russian for fear he'd say the heat had got me and I was seeing things.

We plodded on, both of us walking now, to make the going easier on our horses. Russian continued his grumbling, blaming Cut Tongue for holding us back. It had been almost two days since the horses had drunk good, and their eyes had started to sink back in their heads. I felt like crying, I was so full of misery and blame of myself. I looked off through the heat waves. I opened my eyes wide, then shook my head. I hadn't imagined it. There was that long wall of rock, only now we were almost right up to it.

"Russian! Look!" I gasped, pointing.

Russian shaded his eyes and stared. "What the hell—" he muttered. He looked back the way we'd come and sized up the situation for a long time. There was nothing but barren wasteland.

"It's the end of the world," he said, "and we're dead." He stumbled back to Cut Tongue and looked down at him, then whirled on me. "And he's dead, too! Dammit! We're all dead, and all because of you!"

About that time a strange cry came from Cut Tongue, and he lifted his weak arm, pointing toward the wall of rock. Then he dropped his hand and struggled to draw something in the sand. I kneeled beside him, leaning close for a better look. He drew an arrow with a crooked shaft; the same as the one he had drawn in Shokabob's tent. I got all excited.

"It's the same arrow, Russian!" I blurted out," like the one on the gold band!"

Russian acted like we were both looney. "Crazy ol' coot," he mumbled, ". . . leadin' us here to the edge of nowhere."

I got hold of his arm. "But he's trying ta tell us somethin'!"

He shrugged me off and stormed away. I was right on his trail.

"But, Russian! That's gotta be Crooked Sky! That's what he's tryin' ta tell us. We made it!"

He stopped by his horse and untied his bedroll from behind the saddle.

"What're you goin' to do?" I asked.

He didn't reply but threw the bedroll over his shoulder and kept on walking. I was fit to be tied.

"Russian, we're almost there!" I pleaded. "We're likely right on top of it! And there's water a' waitin' for us . . . and Charlotte . . . and enough gold to make you rich right beyond that wall of rock!"

He stopped in the shade of a big boulder and threw down his bedroll. "In the mornin', if I wake up and my horse ain't dead, I'm headin' back, and I'm takin' that damn headband, too. And you can do as you please."

"You dirty, old drunken coward!" I hollered, so full of mad I could hardly force out the words. "Always givin' up! You're nothin' but a coward! Coward! *Coward!*"

Russian jumped to his feet and plowed me a good one. I didn't know what had hit me as I lay there on the ground, shaking my head, trying to get my wits about me.

"Call me a coward, will you!" he roared. "Why, you ungrateful rascal! After all I've been through fer you!"

He stomped back to his blankets and flopped down with his back against the rock, still ranting.

"Gold! I was a jackass to ever listen to you. All you've brought me is misery and sufferin'!"

I wiped the blood away that oozed from my lip as I struggled to my feet, certain by this time that Russian really hated me. I felt pretty much the same about him right then. He rambled on, hardly taking a breath between oaths.

"Now, we're dead, Sam Sutter! Jest like that sister of yours! Jest like B'ar Killer and ol' Cut Tongue! We're all dead, thanks to you, you ornery, pig-headed —oh, what's the use. Git outa my sight!"

I knew there was no use trying to calm him down. I took off on a run, paying no attention to where I was headed.

". . . And if you and your God can scale that wall of rock," Russian yelled after me, "well, my luck to you!"

I didn't stop running until my breath was gone, and when I pulled up there was that massive cliff right in front of me. I stood gazing up at it, feeling like a twig under a pine tree.

I don't know how long I stumbled along that wall of rock looking for an opening through or an end to it. There was neither one. I felt helpless and sick inside. Russian was right. Old Cut Tongue had led us to the wrong place. I fell on my face in the sand. A bit later, after I'd quit bawling, I rolled over on my back and looked up at the sky. I noticed the buzzards as they wheeled and gathered, dropping lower and lower as they circled. I knew they saw me, and most likely thought I was dying. I didn't waste anymore time. I got to my feet and headed back toward Russian and Cut Tongue.

Chapter Twelve

I couldn't sleep that night. I was up before the sun, standing looking down at Cut Tongue. He lay with his eyes closed, and I wasn't sure if he was alive or dead. I took the gold headband from my belt and kneeled beside him. I pulled his blankets back and hooked it under the wide leather thong he wore around his waist and covered him back up.

"It was meant to be yours," I said, getting back to my feet, "and Russian ain't havin' it, I was hopin' you'd brought us to the right place, and I could take you back to your people like I promised, but I guess Russian's right. You're just a crazy old Injun."

Right then, Cut Tongue opened his eyes wide and gazed up at me like he understood every word I said, then slowly turned his head and stared at the wall of rock. It didn't seem so far away, now. All at once, Cut Tongue started making strange noises, his eyes all excited. I turned to look, and then I saw it! A thin sliver of rising sunlight pierced the granite wall. As I watched, it widened to a shaft several feet wide that flooded the desert floor. I stumbled back in wonderment. There was a way through the wall of rock after all!

"Crooked Sky!" I gasped.

I turned and ran to where Russian still slept. "Russian! Russian! Look!"

He raised up on one elbow and squinted at me. I pointed to the shaft of light coming through the rock.

"It's Crooked Sky!" I said, so excited I could hardly keep from jumping up and down.

Russian got to his feet like someone in a trance and walked toward the cliff, gaping. I was right at his heels, and we stood and watched the sun come up over the rim, then pull its rays from the crevice until it seemed to no longer be there.

"I ain't never seen nothin' like that in all my life," said Russian, shaking his head.

It didn't take long for us to break camp, and a short time later, we inched along the cliff where the shale broke away and sloped to the desert floor. We rode in single file, Russian in the lead followed by Cut Tongue's pony pulling the travois. I came behind, leading the packmule. We paused before the deep crevice in the face of the cliff. It was barely wide enough for a horse and rider to get through, and Russian got off to take a look. I follered him, and we stood gazing up the rugged trail. We could see daylight at the far end, and there was something creepy about it that made my spine tingle.

"I'd never have believed it," said Russian in awe. "It's a freak of nature to behold!"

"But why couldn't we see it before?" I asked.

"I don't know. Somethin' to do with the angle of the sun's rays, I suppose. Well . . . come on. It's a helluva long way to the top."

We got back on our horses and rode into the crevice. It was like riding into a jagged tunnel, and the farther we went the rougher it got. We were getting close to the top when Russian stopped.

"Sounds like water up there," he said.

I cocked my ear for a second. "It is!" I yelled.

By this time, the horses could smell the water and they didn't have to be urged anymore. When we came into the sunlight, it was so bright it almost blinded us. Not far from the opening, a small stream trickled from the rocks above, feeding the pool. The horses jammed their noses into it until their nostrils were covered. Me and Russian flattened ourselves on our bellies and drank like we were going to dry up the whole pool. After I got my fill, I got a cup from our supplies and filled it a couple of times for the old Indian. I didn't think he was in much shape to drink, but he fooled me. When I lifted his head and put the cup to his lips, he grabbed it with both of his shaky old hands and gulped down the whole thing. I could tell he was happy to be on familiar ground.

When I looked up, Russian was still in the pool with all of his clothes on. He was slinging water every which way, and hollering loud enough to scare the eagles out of their nests.

"Ain't it beautiful?" he yelled. "Ain't it so-oo bea-uu-ti-ful?"

I couldn't help but laugh the way he carried on, and it didn't take me long to jump right in there with him.

Later, as our clothes were drying, we wandered around in our long johns looking things over a bit. It seemed we were on top of the world. Standing on a wide shelf of rock, we gazed over the rugged canyons and wide valleys rimmed with high, grass-covered mesas.

"Ain't it somethin'," I said, "hid off here in the middle of nowhere?"

"One more freak of nature," said Russian, "after all of that desert."

Then something caught his eye. He moved out farther on the shelf of rock. His lower jaw dropped like it was falling off his face. He went to the ground on one knee and motioned me over. I stared. Embedded in the rock was a gold arrow, its shaft zigzagging like a bolt of lightning.

Russian leaped to his feet yelling, "Gold! Gold!
I'm gonna be rich!"

He grabbed me and swung me around in the air.
"Ya done me right, boy!" he shouted. "Ya brung me
to the rainbow's end! Ain't it beautiful? Sweet, yeller
gold!"

Then he got down on his knees over the arrow
and kissed it a couple of times. When he acted like
that, I didn't have much use for him. He carried on,
snorting and drooling like it was something good to
eat. I didn't want to see anymore, so I turned toward
the flat stone that overhung the precipice.

"We'll share it, Sam!" Russian was still fussing
over the arrow. "This, and whatever we find. There'll
be plenty for both of us, you can bet on thet.
OOOooohhheeee! Sweet yeller gold!"

I stared down at the flat rock, then shivered.
"Come look at this!" I called to Russian.

He got up and hurried over. "What did you find,
boy? More of it, already? You know, I figure Cut
Tongue's whole tribe must wear gold crowns, and—"

He stopped all together.

"What is it?" I asked again.

Russian stooped to examine the dark stain that
covered the stone, a strange look crossing his face. He
gazed back toward the old Indian.

"If ol' Cut Tongue could talk, I'll bet he'd have
a tale or two ta tell about this," he said, shaking his
head.

"What is it?" I asked.

"Ain't you ever seen human blood before?"

I felt a little sick. "Human blood?" I gasped.

"No tellin' how many have been butchered right
here on this spot . . . then pushed off into the clouds."

I shuddered, then stepped to the edge of the

71

gorge and carefully looked down. Feeling dizzy, I pulled back right quick.

"Human sacrifices?" I asked Russian. "Why would they do that?"

"Damned if I know."

He turned toward the rocks where our clothes were drying. He stopped short, and together we gazed in wonder. Looming up before us, and behind the pool of water, a shaft of rock looked like it had been pushed right out of the mountain at a strange, tilted angle a hundred or more feet in the air. The top of it was so sharp, it made me think of a church steeple. Russian moved toward it.

"The way the durn thing tips, it's like it was most ready to tumble over," he said.

"Crooked Sky," I said, ". . . it must be the reason they named it that!"

"Come on, boy," said Russian. "Let's dig out that gold arrow and git to packin', or who knows—"

He stopped, gaping, as four Indians rose up like they'd been shot out of the ground. They had both of our rifles, and pointed them at our hearts like they meant business.

"Humph! Well, fit to be scalped!" exclaimed Russian. "If this ain't embarrassin'! And not as much as a bowie knife ta lay my hands on."

Those Indians were dressed just like the ones that stole Charlotte, and I knew they had to belong to the same tribe. The looked so cussed fierce, my feet froze right to the ground. They motioned with the rifle barrels, and Russian looked from them to me.

"Well, prayin' boy," he said, "git to your prayers. 'Cause we sure as hell need 'em. Now!"

Chapter Thirteen

I could tell Russian's pride was mighty hurt when two of those Indians put ropes around our necks and, riding our horses, pulled us along like a couple of balky mules. Still in our long johns, and carrying our clothes, we hopped and skipped over the rough ground trying to keep up with them. Russian cursed them at the top of his voice with every breath. Once he got hung up in some brambles and went to barking at them, until he got such a hard jerk he nearly fell on his face.

"Why, you dirty . . . !" he stormed. "Ain't no Injun *ever* done nothin' like this to me. I swear . . . you ain't gonna git away with it!"

"Russian," I said, as I trotted along beside him, "you gotta make 'em understand who we are!"

"There ain't no Injun tongue left to try," he grumbled.

The Indian gave him another hard tug with the rope.

"Why, you durn jackass!" Russian howled. ". . . Sittin' on my horse like ya owned 'im! Wait'll I flatten your face between a couple of boulders, you ugly son of a—!"

All of his threats didn't seem to put much scare into those Indians, and they kept right on dragging us. I gave a quick glance back over my shoulder to see what had happened to Cut Tongue. One of the Indians was riding his pony and pulling the travois behind. The other followed on our packmule.

We finally came to a well-traveled trail, and it was

easier on our bare feet. It was lined with boulders and trees and, for some reason, I suddenly got a creepy feeling in my spine. In a minute, I could see why. Indians stared at us from a hundred places behind trees and rocks. Seeing we were captives, we expected them to yell or run after us, but they stood like fence posts, hardly moving an eyelid. I noticed there were few children among them.

Soon we came to a long, oval clearing that was completely surrounded by trees. It was filled with strange dwellings made of stone, set here and there at different levels on little rises of ground.

The braves leading us stopped and got off their horses. They lowered Cut Tongue's travois to the ground, then took the ropes from our necks and tied us up against a tree. They disappeared with our horses, leaving us to be gawked at by the other Indians.

"They ain't gonna kill us, are they, Russian?" I asked.

"How in the hell do I know?" he snapped. "I keep askin' myself . . . what the devil am I doin' here?"

When an old squaw leaned over me and grinned down with her pointed, snagged teeth, I wished the ground would swaller me up. She had long hair that looked like dirty straw, and a face so wrinkled she put me in mind of a dried-up prune. She moved over to Russian with a cunning gleam in her eye, and I noticed the small, earthen dish in her hand. She stirred something in it with her fingers, and when she raised them for a sniff, I could see it was some sort of slimy, green, jelly-like stuff that made me sick to look at it. It must have affected Russian the same way, because he started to cough and gag, and about that time she slapped a whole handful of it into his mouth. He tried to spew it out and she clamped her hand over

74

his nose and mouth, forcing him to swaller it. He strangled and flopped around like a fish on a river bank. She finally got it down him, then turned to me.

"Keep your mouth shut, boy!" warned Russian, still gagging and sputtering. "She's tryin' to poison us!"

I turned my face away, and when she came close I tried to kick her. She never would have got that stuff down me but for the young squaw that came to help her. When she tried to pry my mouth open, I did my best to bite her fingers. She finally had to use a stick, and the old woman stuffed the paste between my teeth and pinched my nostrils and covered my mouth like she had Russian's. There was nothing I could do but swaller it.

"Damn you, kid," Russian yelped. "You took it!"

"What else would you have me do?"

"Well . . . we're poisoned, fer shore. It's jest a matter of time and we'll both be dead."

I looked away as two Indian braves stepped from the biggest lodge in the village and came toward us. One was a lot older than the other, but they were both dressed in fine clothes. As they drew near, the younger one fell behind and I couldn't get a good look at him. Russian began to fuss and moan, and I got to worrying about what was happening to him. If we both died, like he said, then what would become of Charlotte?

"Oh, I'm goin'!" Russian whined, his eyes getting bleary. "I'm on my way out, and here I could be trappin' in that Ol' Smoky country with B'ar Killer. Instead, I'm a' layin' here dead, near naked . . . an' bein' gawked at by a buncha squaws . . . !"

I could see he struggled to keep his wits about him, and was having a hard time to focus his eyes on those two Indians coming toward us. With his back to me, the younger brave stepped to Cut Tongue and bent to loosen the thongs that bound the old man's blankets. The chief stood on the far side where I could get a good look at him. His head was shaved, and he had all sorts of gold ornaments on his neck and arms. When he saw me watching him, his eyes bored right through me, and sure gave me the shivers. When the younger one pulled back Cut Tongue's blanket, the old man's eyes were closed, and he clutched the gold band to his chest. The chief stared, then leaned over him for a closer look.

"Eckimah!" he gasped, then drew back, a wild look of fear on his face.

Cut Tongue slowly opened his eyes and gazed up at the chief. I could see he recognized him immediately, and his face went to writhing like a wounded snake. All at once, he lifted the headband in his shaking fingers and waved it in the chief's face, making the most terrible sounds I had ever heard. From the dark looks they gave each other, I could tell there was sure bad blood between them. The chief stepped forward again, and Cut Tongue shrank back like a big scare went through him. And it sure had me wondering. The young brave got to his feet, looking from one to the other in a confused way as more Indians began to crowd around. I glanced at Russian to see if he had taken it all in, and he looked puzzled, like he was trying hard to figure it out. All at once, I started to get a queer feeling, and I set my eyes on the gold band Cut Tongue was still waving and yelling about. Then the world started spinning around me, and everything went black.

Chapter Fourteen

I don't know how much time went by before I began to hear or feel anything again, but it must have been quite a while. Wailing sounds came from what seemed like a million voices as I tried to struggle out of my nightmare. I couldn't even remember where I was, and my throat was dry, and I shivered in a cold sweat. When I got my wits about me, I raised up on my elbow and looked around. Things were foggy for a few minutes, then I began to piece together what had happened. Russian was still unconscious beside me, and I was surprised to see we both had been untied, but Cut Tongue was gone.

I sat up and gazed toward the center of the clearing where all the sounds were coming from. A big fire raged, lighting up the whole Indian village. At the side of the fire, a platform was raised, and I jumped when I saw Cut Tongue lying on it. My first thought was they were going to burn him alive. Then I could see he was all decked out in finery, and I was sure he must be dead. The chief, dressed in more fancy clothes and feathers, stood beside him, chanting in a sing-song voice as he lifted his face to the rising flames. It looked like the whole tribe had gathered near the fire.

Russian started to groan, and I crawled over to him and gave him a nudge.

"Russian! . . . Russian! Wake up!"

He groaned again, and I shook him hard by the shoulder.

"Look!" I told him. "They've untied us."

Russian slowly sat up, holding his head.

"Oh . . . I feel like the inside of a sow's belly," he moaned. Then he saw the fire. "What the devil—!"

"It's old Cut Tongue," I said. "He must be dead, and they're havin' some kind of a ceremony."

"Looks like they're fixin' to barbecue 'im . . . an' most likely, we'll be next. Well, I ain't waitin' 'round to find out. Come on!"

We started to crawl on our hands and knees toward the trees on the outside of the clearing. We didn't get far before three pair of moccasined feet stopped us. We looked into the stern faces of three braves, and they jerked us to our feet, marching us over to the fire. Still guarding us from behind, they stopped beside the Indians watching the ceremony.

The chief cried out in an eerie wail as the Indians from the sidelines brought him bright ornaments and colored feathers to put on Cut Tongue's body. I quit paying attention to what he was doing and looked around for Charlotte. All of the Indian women looked alike to me, and, there was no sign of my sister.

"They burn Eckimah . . . soon . . . in flames."

I almost jumped out of my long johns, and me and Russian both whirled in surprise to hear someone speaking our language. A pretty, young Indian girl, about sixteen or so, stood at my shoulder. Her eyes were soft and brown like a young doe's as she stared into the fire.

"Who are you?" I asked.

She still didn't look my way.

"Me Ashkea . . . daughter to Chief Shumeki," she said. "We honor Eckimah, his brother. . . . Great warrior. . . . Much loved by people. . . . Lost many years. My father feel much sorrow. . . . Now brother return, Chief Shumeki very angry . . . for one who kill Eckimah."

Me and Russian both stared at her.

"Kill him!" exclaimed Russian. "You mean Ol' Cut Tongue's the chief's brother, and somebudy killed 'im?"

We glanced at each other, wondering when all of this could have taken place, but before she could reply the chief's voice rose in a wail that lifted the hair on the back of my neck. He still heaped all kinds of fancy stuff on old Cut Tongue's body.

"Eckimah . . . once to be chief," Ashkea went on. "But fail test at Crooked Sky. Young brother, Shumeki . . . win gold . . . become chief."

I stared at her. "No! That ain't right! He passed the test." I turned to the trapper. "Didn't he, Russian? That's why he cried when he saw the gold band."

"Shumeki win gold . . . not Eckimah," insisted Ashkea, and I could tell she didn't like me telling her what was what. "Shumeki become chief. Eckimah feel great shame . . . leave people . . . never return."

I couldn't figure that one out, and I turned to Russian, but he was gazing off at Cut Tongue.

"Royal blood," he muttered, "and all these years a' livin' the life of a squaw."

Shumeki directed two braves with long poles to push the platform holding Cut Tongue's body into the fire, and a howl went up from the crowd that sounded like a pack of wolves on a winter's night.

"We jest might be next, boy," Russian said to me.

I looked at Ashkea and she, too, was watching the flames. I stepped around in front of her.

"Look, whoever you are," I said to her, "you've gotta help me. Your people stole . . . took my sister."

I poked my chest with my finger to help her understand what I was saying. She went right on staring at the fire like she hadn't heard a word I said, then I saw the tears sliding down her cheeks. Her eyes were on a young brave coming toward the fire from the far side. I recognized him at once as the one who had kneeled at Cut Tongue's side and pulled back his blanket. Now I got a good look at him. The first thing I saw was Cut Tongue's gold band on his head, and I knew that he was the one that had stole Charlotte. All excited, I whirled on Russian.

"That's him! The one with the gold band!" I yelled. "He's the one that took Charlotte! Russian, he's the one!"

Russian grabbed me, trying to calm me down. "Now, jest take it easy, boy. You aimin' to take on the whole tribe?"

I didn't say anything for a minute, staring first at Ashkea, then the Indian brave with the headband.

"He Ashkea's brother . . . Temkai," she said, still gazing straight ahead. "Must wear gold . . . soon to be chief."

"Then he has my sister, and I've got to see her!" I cried. Then, feeling the tears stinging my eyes, I pleaded, "Ashkea, you've gotta help me, please!"

"Little brother," she said, her voice soft and tender. "Ashkea cry, too. Cheimish like sister. Many moons, she teach of her ways . . . I teach her to be good wife . . . to Temkai."

"Wife! You mean, that's why he stole her?"

"Many years tribe grow smaller. No strong babies to make great warriors. Need new blood . . . new squaws. Cheimish do fine . . . love Temkai." Her face twisted like she was filled with great pain. "Now . . . she must die."

Wide-eyed, I stared at her, too stunned to say a word for a few seconds.

"Die!" I finally gasped out, looking from her to Russian—and saw he was as shocked as me.

Ashkea still gazed across the fire, and the tears were really running down her face. None of it made any sense to me. I follered her stare. It was the first

80

time I'd seen the light-haired girl standing there. Her head was bowed, her clothes dirty and torn. The flames leaped higher, and I couldn't see her very well. I craned my neck for a better look. The fire died down for a second, and she raised her head. It was my sister!

"Charlotte!" I cried out.

Hearing my voice, she straightened, searching for the one who called her name.

"They say . . . she take life of Eckimah," whispered Ashkea.

I whirled on her. "Killed old Cut Tongue? No! She wouldn't do that!" I headed for the fire, yelling out, "Charlotte! Charlotte!"

Charlotte saw me as the two braves behind me jerked me back. I went to kicking and slugging them with all I had. They finally held me so I couldn't move a muscle. Charlotte kept trying to break loose from the squaws that guarded her. I could see her hands were tied behind her, but her body reached out to me, pleading for help. Her face twisted in anguish as the squaws started to pull her away. I turned to Ashkea, but her eyes, filled with hopeless pity, were still on Charlotte. Then one of the squaws pulled a leather hood over my sister's head, and they dragged her off into the shadows and out of sight.

Chapter Fifteen

I guess there comes a time in a boy's life when he has to grow up pretty fast, and I sure did a lot of it that night. After much pleading, I finally convinced Ashkea that me and Russian ought to have a talk with her father. Before long, we were dressed and sat in the chief's lodge in front of him and his council. Russian and Ashkea sat on each side of me, and she acted as our interpreter. Shumeki and his council just stared at us, not saying a thing. I'll never forget how cold and hard Shumeki looked, and I was so full of scare I could hardly keep from jumping up and ducking out of there. Temkai sat next to his father, his face grim, but every once in a while, he gave me a soft glance that told me he understood how I felt. Finally, I couldn't stand it any longer, and turned to Ashkea.

"I've gotta see my sister," I said, "Please . . . !"

"Ashkea sorry," she replied, giving Temkai a quick glance, and I noticed the pain that crossed his face. "Chief's law say . . . no one speak with Cheimish."

"But she didn't kill that old man and you know it. He was nearly dead, anyway!"

"My father say . . . while Eckimah rest in lodge, Cheimish come with knife . . . kill him," said Ashkea. "Shumeki hear cries . . . come to save brother . . . but too late."

"But she couldn't have!" I cried. "She had no reason. You're her friend. Tell your father she didn't do it."

Ashkea spoke a few words to Shumeki, and he muttered something back to her.

"Father say . . . he speak truth," she said.

"Now, see here—" I began, but Russian cut me off.

"Let me handle this, Sam." He turned to Ashkea. "Now, listen to me, miss. Tell that father of yours we come here as friends. We brung back his lost brother, riskin' our lives doin' it, an' all we ask in return is to take a lil' gold and go in peace."

"Russian!" I exclaimed, wishing there was some way I could strangle him.

He glared at me. "First things first, boy, and you promised me gold, remember?"

"My sister comes first!" I shouted at him. "You greedy old—"

"All right, all right," he tried to calm me down, then turned to Ashkea. "Tell your father to let this boy's sister go, and give us some gold, and we'll be on our way."

Ashkea spoke to her father in their native tongue. Shumeki replied, looking at me, then Russian, his expression never changing. Ashkea turned to Russian.

"Chief Shumeki say . . . you bring lost brother home . . . you and boy go in peace."

"What about the gold?" asked Russian, and I wanted to knock his head off.

"There is no gold," replied Ashkea.

Old Russian really exploded then. "What do you mean, no gold? Thet crown your brother's wearin' and thet arrow on those rocks up there ain't made of tin!"

"Ancient gold in tribe from very first," said Ashkea. "Old ones bring . . . when come from land . . . far away."

"You tryin' to tell me that all the gold left here is what's up at Crooked Sky," growled Russian. "Well, I don't believe it!"

By this time, I'd lost all patience with him and

83

jumped to my feet so full of mad I felt like chunking him on the head with a piece of wood.

"Serves you right, you greedy old drunk, thinkin' about gold at a time like this!" I turned to Ashkea, trying to put down the lump in my throat. "What about my sister?"

She looked at me for a long time, and tears filled her eyes.

"Father say . . . to pay for crime against tribe, Cheimish must die."

I glared at the old chief and felt like tearing into him, but I knew that wouldn't help Charlotte none.

"But she didn't do it, Ashkea. I know she didn't! Tell him!" I pleaded.

Shumeki stood up and said something to Ashkea.

"Chief all finished," she told us. "No more to say."

Russian got to his feet. "Come on, boy, let's discuss this outside." He took hold of my arm but I jerked away, glaring again at Shumeki, then Ashkea.

"I ain't gonna let 'er die!" I yelled. "You tell that old buzzard of a chief that if he tries to kill her, I'm gonna kill him! Now tell him that for a start, 'cause I mean business!"

Russian looked nervously around. "You lookin' to git us barbecued?" He glanced at Ashkea. "OOOooo-hhheee! She's tellin' 'im!"

As Ashkea spoke to Shumeki, raged boiled up in his face. He glared down at me like he was going to choke me, but I stood my ground.

"Chief angry," said Ashkea. "No like being called . . . old buzzard. He say . . . you go now . . . or die with girl."

"You tell 'im I'm not leavin' without my sister!"

Russian grabbed hold of me again to drag me out. "Will you shet your mouth?" he said through clenched teeth.

"No!" I fired back at him, so mad I could fight a barrel of wildcats. "I didn't come all this way to see my sister die! And before I give up fightin' for Charlotte's life, I'll give my own first. You tell him that, Ashkea!"

"I ain't seen nothin' like you in all my days!" moaned Russian, rolling his eyes back in his head. "You've gone clean crazy!"

Shumeki spoke sharply to Ashkea, I guess wanting to know what we were saying. Ashkea turned to him and his council. They talked back and forth for a few minutes, then Shumeki's voice got harsh, and Ashkea started, staring at him. She turned to me with a strange look on her face.

"Will he let her go?" I asked.

"He say . . . if Cheimish have no blame . . . boy must prove. Must race sun . . . give blood . . . die . . . to let sister live."

That sure took my breath away. For a minute, I didn't know what to say or do. I looked at the chief's stony face, then at Temkai and the rest of the council still sitting on the floor. Temkai, looking awful troubled, got slowly to his feet. The other council members didn't budge but just sat staring at me to see how I'd take that. I turned to Russian for help. He looked at me with scorn.

"Try to wiggle outa this one, prayin' boy," he said. "So God's behind you, is he? Well . . . this is a damn big order! Even from God!"

I ducked my head and thought for a bit. I looked at the ring of stern faces gazing at me, then took a deep breath and turned to the Indian girl.

"Tell me, Ashkea," I said. "What do I have to do?"

Chapter Sixteen

Me and Russian left the chief's lodge a few minutes later, and I felt all dried up and numb inside. We walked side by side, and Russian kept up a steady string of talk, but my mind was so jumbled nothing made any sense.

"Race the sun!" Russian was saying. "Damnedest blood-thirsty game I ever heerd of . . . expectin' a scrawny kid like you to race the sun, and all for the privilege of receivin' an arrow meant for your sister."

"We gotta find out who did it, Russian," I told him. "That's the only answer. We gotta find out and prove it!"

Russian laughed. "You fool kid . . . haven't you figured that one out yet?"

I looked at him in surprise. "*You* know?"

"I'm not so blind I can't see the facts," he replied. "If ol' Cut Tongue was tellin' the truth about passin' the test and winnin' the gold band, then he should've been the chief, right? All I know is that he was left out in the desert without a tongue to die . . . and now, someone else is boss here in his place."

I stopped and stared at him. All at once it hit me like someone had rolled a rock off a cliff on my head. "You mean, *Shumeki?*" I gasped.

Russian grabbed me and looked nervously around. "Shut your mouth, boy," he said, "or we ain't worth rags . . . not to ourselves, your sister, or *nobody!*"

"So now what do we do?"

"Hell if I know."

"We gotta help her escape!"

"Damn! You do expect miracles, don't you?"

We walked on and didn't say anymore for a minute or two, then Russian continued, "Where's all that gold you promised me, huh? The bargain bein' I was to bring you here for the gold, and now you're askin' me to risk my life instead."

I didn't know what to say to that. I guess my face showed how disappointed and miserable I was, and Russian repented a little.

"Well . . . maybe I'll think about it," he said.

"We ain't got time to think!" I flared. "We only got 'til mornin'!"

Russian looked at me plumb exasperated. "I said I'd think about it, didn't I?"

I felt so let down, I took off on a run, and didn't look back until I was clear out of the village. I cut up a steep bank and headed off through the trees. I guess I'd been running yet if I hadn't tripped on some bear grass and fell. I sat up panting for breath, the blood beating so hard in my head I couldn't find my right mind. I crawled to a tree and leaned in to it.

"It ain't fair, God!" I cried out, bitter at everyone for what happened. "Ain't I given enough already? Ain't Pa and Ma, and all of us? And now, you're askin' too much . . . and I don't know if I can do it . . . if I've even got the courage."

I choked and blubbered there for a bit, fighting against what was going on inside of me. It would be no easy thing for me to give my life for someone, even my sister—though I was sure she'd do the same for me. The thought of it put such a scare in me, I almost wished I was dead already.

"Please, God, give me courage," I said. "I just can't let Charlotte die!"

It wasn't long after that I began to feel better,

and I sat down with my back to the tree and stared out into the night. Whatever it took, I had to do it. In the morning I'd tell the chief I was ready.

"Little brother." Ashkea's voice came so soft I could hardly hear it. I turned to see her standing in the shadows a few feet away. I didn't answer, thinking maybe she'd go away. I didn't want her to know I'd been crying.

The Indian girl spoke again. "Ashkea sorry . . . she come to share your grief."

I still didn't reply, and she stepped from the shadows into the light of the moon.

"Little brother . . . brave warrior," she said. "Have good heart . . . show great love for sister."

"Gosh durn it!" I said, "and look what I brung on her! And my poor ma and pa! They've prob'ly give me up for dead, too. Ashkea, there's gotta be a way to get Charlotte free. Won't you help me?"

"My father's laws very hard. If Ashkea turn against him, he—" She didn't finish but shook her head sadly.

"Then what about Temaki? He's her husband. He could do somethin'!"

"You not see, little brother? Temkai, too, must obey father's law. He bound by honor . . . of ancient gold."

"Does that mean more to him than Charlotte? Doesn't he love her enough to speak up to that old chief for what's right?"

She didn't say anything for so long I figured I'd made her mad, and she wouldn't help me now no matter how much I begged. I felt like everybody had let me down, even God.

Then Ashkea held out her hand and gave me a little smile. "Please, little brother . . . come . . ."

She led me back to the edge of the village, then stopped. We stood for a bit while she listened and searched the shadows. I could see Russian sitting in the light of the fire across the clearing. He was up to something, but we were so far away, I couldn't tell what. Ashkea motioned me on, and we slipped through the rocks and trees. As we got closer, I got a better look at the old trapper. He was guzzling something from a gourd, screwing up his face into every shape you could imagine. Then he'd squirm and holler like a bunch of ants were stinging him. The old hag who had doped us earlier was grinning and cackling at him like she was getting an awful big kick out of his antics. Other Indians watched from close by, and they all were laughing like he sure tickled them, too.

Ashkea motioned me again to foller her. We slipped in and out among trees and lodges, then she stopped and pointed to a dwelling that was guarded in front by two braves.

"They keep Cheimish there," she said.

She put her hand on my arm, warning me to be quiet as we sneaked through the rocks and bushes to the back of Charlotte's dwelling. Ashkea stopped again to listen. I couldn't hear a sound but Russian laughing and hollering across the clearing. We crept up to a small opening in the back of the dwelling that was too small for me to even get my head in. Ashkea peered inside, saying something in her own tongue. I heard a whimpering cry and a small rustling sound, then Charlotte's face appeared in the opening.

"Charlotte!" I whispered, squeezing in as close as I could, but scared to death of what might happen if we got caught.

She reached out and touched my face with her fingers, sobbing my name over and over. I started to cry, and Ashkea had tears running down her face, too.

"Charlotte . . . why have you—you gotta die?" I could hardly force out the words. "I don't un-understand!"

"They think I killed the chief's brother, Sam . . . the one you brought back," she whimpered between sobs. ". . . But I didn't . . . I didn't!"

"What happened that they would blame you?" I asked.

"Some of the people told me you and your friend had been captured, and I was comin' to try to help you. When I passed by the lodge next to Chief Shumeki's, I heard cries comin' from inside. I was sure it must be the two of you, and I slipped to the window to see what was happenin'. I saw a figure bending over the man I thought must be your friend." She gave Ashkea a quick look, her face really worried, then went on. "After he left, I saw the knife in the man's chest, and he still moaned, tryin' to pull it out. I ran into the lodge and jerked it out just as Shumeki came in with his braves. He was very angry with me and insisted I killed his brother, Eckimah."

"But you didn't. You had no reason!"

"It is my word against the chief's."

"And the man you saw do it, who was he?"

Charlotte bowed her head. "He cannot be accused."

"But why? You saw him!"

"No one will believe me."

"Tell me! I'll make 'em believe it!"

Charlotte had a hopeless look about her. "It's no use, Sam," she said. "That is why they wouldn't let you see me. If they thought you knew, you would have to die, too."

I turned to the Indian girl. "Can't you do something, Ashkea? You know who killed your uncle, don't you?"

Ashkea's eyes were full of fear. She turned her back and put her face in her hands, sobbing. Then I thought of Russian and what he said to me about Shumeki in front of the chief's lodge. I got so full of mad I felt like screaming.

"I know who did it!" I hissed. "Don't worry, Charlotte, everything's gonna be all right. You just leave it to me."

"Please, Sam," she pleaded, "I want you to go home before they harm you."

"I'm going all right, but I'm taking you with me."

"Sam, there's no way—"

I cut her off. "Then me and Russian will figure one out."

It was like when I spoke Russian's name, he popped into the picture. We could hear a lot of racket, and Ashkea and I went to peek around the corner of the dwelling. Russian had the guards' attention as he crossed the clearing, singing at the top of his voice, so stoned drunk he could hardly walk. The old, toothless hag followed him, still giggling and packing the gourd he'd been boozing from. He stopped and took it from her for another swig, then between belches his voice came to us loud and clear through the still night.

"Nastiest stuff I ever tasted," he lamented, "but, damn, it's good! Ya know how I know if it's good? It's the feelin' I git. Yessir! Ooohhheee! First comes that shiver enough ta freeze the hair on a b'ar's rear end . . . Then comes thet sweet, warm feelin' crawlin' right up through my toes an' into my spine, and it feels *so* good." He turned to pinch the old hag's cheek. "Ya know, honey, you're gittin' purtier all the time!"

91

I had never been so disgusted with that old trapper. Here he was, drunk clear out of his head when I needed him the most.

He stopped by a small pool of water near the front of Charlotte's dwelling and surprised me by kneeling down and dousing his head and face good with it. He got up and shook himself like a wet dog and grinned at the old hag. He spatted his hands together.

"Now, honey, I'm ready!" he said.

I couldn't figure out what he was ready for but I found out in just a few minutes. When he walked up to the guards, they didn't seem in the least concerned. I guess they thought he was too drunk to do anything. He even surprised me when all of a sudden he tore into them like a mad bull elk. First thing he did was take a slug at one, and when the other came at him he kicked him in the belly with his boot heel, sprawling him on the ground. I realized the old trapper wasn't as drunk as he pretended when he got down to really giving them a fight. He punched the first one a good one, a time or two, then got a head-lock on him. When the other got to his feet and moved in, Russian made another pass at him with his boot again, and lost his footing and fell to the ground. The two braves piled on top of him. My first impulse was to get out there and help him, but Ashkea pulled me back, shaking her head, and I knew then I'd only make matters worse.

By this time, Russian was wailing for B'ar Killer and cursing the two Indians.

"You dirty curs!" he yelped. "You wouldn't be doin' this to me if ol' B'ar killer was here! I oughta slit your throats!"

Hearing the commotion, other Indians came running to see what was going on. Ashkea took hold of me.

"Hurry, little brother . . . they must not find you here."

We went back where Charlotte still stood at the opening. She handed me something, and in the moonlight I could see it was her Bible.

"I want you to take this and go home to Ma and Pa," she said, "Please, Sam, do as I say."

Even though Ma had always told me to mind Charlotte, this was one time I didn't intend to.

"I'm comin' back for you, Charlotte," I whispered.

More clatter started up out in front, and I could hear Russian grumbling as the Indians marched him away.

"Please, Sam, go before it's too late," Charlotte urged me, then turned to the Indian girl. "And Ashkea, keep my secret. Temkai must never know that—well, you know, not with what he must do?"

Ashkea nodded, and I looked from one to the other, trying to figure out what my sister meant. Before I could ask, Ashkea grabbed me and pulled me off into the shadows. She hesitated just a moment to see which way the Indians were headed with Russian. It was sure a surprise to me to see they had let him go, and he was staggering off toward our pile of gear, grumbling as he went. The old hag still follered him faithfully behind.

"He was my only hope," I said to Ashkea, feeling as let down as a man hanging in a noose, "but I guess he did the best he could."

With a big sigh, I turned to the Indian girl. "What does it mean, Ashkea, to race the sun?"

She looked at me for a long time, her eyes big and sad, then she said, "Come, little brother . . . I will show you."

Once again, we ducked into the shadows and slipped off into the night.

Chapter Seventeen

I don't guess I'll ever forget that beautiful, wild land Ashkea showed me that night as she stood on the edge of a rocky precipice, the wind whipping her hair and clothing. She pointed to distant peaks that were set here and there like giant salt and pepper shakers on flat, round tables. I could see the moonlight shining through rainbow arches of stone. Canyon after canyon opened up into flat country, then broke off at the edges like a piece of cake into rugged cliffs and more canyons. It put a scare into me that made me dizzy, and I couldn't push it down. Ashkea kept telling me over and over what I must do. The more she talked, the more shivery I got.

Finally, I said, "But, Ashkea how could anybody ever do it?"

"Even strongest warriors fail test at Crooked Sky."

This didn't make me feel any better, and I guess I showed it. She turned to me, her eyes pleading.

"Please, little brother . . . do as sister begs," she said. "Go home to own land . . . to mother and father. Ashkea fears for you . . . and Cheimish."

I was too overcome to answer right away, but gazed off through the moonlight. A hazy mist covered the canyons, making them look eerie and mysterious. Then, about fifty yards away, I saw a figure standing on a rocky point. It startled me so I turned to Ashkea and knew at once she had seen it, too.

"Temkai," she said. "My brother very sad . . . for what he must do."

"What's that?" I asked. "I don't understand."

She hesitated like she didn't want to tell me.

"I've got to know, Ashkea," I insisted.

"Because he wears ancient gold . . . his arrow must take life of Cheimish."

I was so stunned for a minute, I couldn't say a word. Then I yelled, "What are you saying?"

She looked uncomfortable. "Our people's ways . . . very hard."

I was so mad I think my face turned purple. "You mean that old chief's ways are hard!" I cried. "He's to blame for all of this!"

Her face looked full of hurt. "Little brother . . . please believe . . . Law has been in tribe for many years . . . from very first."

"They're crazy laws—" I began, then all at once made myself realize there was nothing I could do to change these people and their silly ways. I was just wasting time, and the only way I could save Charlotte was to give my life for hers. I whirled on Ashkea, and she jumped like she thought I was going to hit her.

"I will do it!" I cried out. "I'll be the one to take Temkai's arrow! Who says I can't make it. God'll help me, and I'll do it, too!"

Ashkea stared at me like she couldn't believe I really meant it.

"You give so much for sister? Ashkea not understand . . . such love."

"She'd do the same for me, and so would Ma and Pa," I told her, holding out Charlotte's Bible. " 'Cause we all believe what it says in here . . . about giving your life for a friend."

When I put the Bible in her hand, she gazed at it for a long time.

"You keep it," I said. "There's no need of me having it now."

95

I could see she was sure suffering. Then a strange, haunting expression crossed her face, sort of sad and confused, and when she raised her head I saw there were tears in her eyes.

"Ashkea feel . . . great shame . . ." she said, then turned and ran down the hill out of sight.

I looked across at Temkai. He still stood as before, but now his eyes were fixed on me, and I wondered just how much he knew and understood of what had gone on between me and his sister.

Chapter Eighteen

By the time I got back to the village and got into my blankets, there wasn't much left of the night, but it still seemed morning would never come. When it fianlly did, Ashkea brought me a breechcloth made of some sort of fine material, and a pair of moccasins she had gotten from a brave. She reminded me again of what would take place and what I must do. I was still so scared I couldn't stand to think about it. When Ashkea left me, she gave me a little smile of encouragement.

"Ashkea wish best . . . for little brother," she said, and I noticed how sad she seemed.

Russian was still sleeping off his booze and hurt pride from the night before, and I didn't bother him. I knew he'd try to change my mind, and it was too late for that now. I slipped out of camp, and a short time before sunup, I stood looking over the stretch of country where I had to race the sun. No land ever seemed so big, so rough or so wide. I thought a bit about Ma and Pa and home, and they all seemed so far away. I was so lonely, it was like a big hand squeezed my heart until it ached something awful. The silence was scary, and I began to wish I'd brought Russian with me. The wind moaned and whispered through the rocks and trees like ghosts in Grandma Sutter's attic that Pa always told about. I watched the sun rays uneasily as they moved down the far-off peak of Crooked Sky. When I saw two Indians standing on the top of a hill a few hundred yards away, I knew it wouldn't be long until the signal came. My heart began to pound in my chest like it was going to beat all of my breath away. My knees got so weak and my mouth so dry, my tongue stuck to the roof like a mud-dobber's nest on the eaves of our cabin back home.

From where I stood, I couldn't see the village, but Indians began to line the trail to Crooked Sky summit like sparrows on a fence. Shumeki already stood at the sacrificial rock facing me, and a short distance away from him, the towering rock of Crooked Sky rose up. At its base, I could see Charlotte with her head covered and her shoulders drooping in despair. Temkai stood tall and straight at her side. They were all so far away they looked like tiny dolls, and I wished I only had to run straight across to them. But that wasn't the way Ashkea told me it had to be done—all of the things she explained to me the night before. I was to run in a wide circle among the canyons and gullies, over hills and through streams, up steep ledges and sheer cliffs. I looked for her now, but there was no sign of her. I wondered, too, where Russian was. If I figured that old trapper right, he'd be wandering through the village, half stoned and searching all over for me. Or maybe he'd gotten disgusted with everything and gotten his horse and headed home.

Three-quarters of the sun became visible as it rose above the mountains, and I could see Chief Shumeki raise his arm to the sky. When the sun came into full view, he sliced his arm down, and his long, moaning wail trembled and echoed across the canyons. It was picked up by the Indian sentinel on the nearest ridge to him and sent on to the next. The signal was carried on and on until it echoed and rolled through the sky. The two Indians nearest me seemed awful anxious as they waited and, when the cry reached them, one raised his spear in the air and yelled long and loud. I took off like an arrow shot from a bow, plenty determined I was going to reach Crooked Sky in time to give my life for my sister.

The earth was hard beneath my feet, and I still moved at a steady pace. I ran into sunlight the mountain shadows had left behind. I leaped over rocks and bushes, zigzagged through tall brush, washes and gullies. My breath still seemed strong enough, but I kept reminding myself of what Ashkea had told me.

"Race the sun," she had said, ". . . not too fast . . . tire too soon. Race the sun . . ."

Already, I was beginning to see how great this test was going to be. Maybe I should have gone home like Charlotte and Ashkea had begged me to.

"I'll make it," I told myself. "I'll show 'em I can."

A sandy hill came up in front of me, and I started to climb it instead of going around it. The deep sand sucked at my feet, slowing down my stride. My breath was coming harder, and sweat was running down my face. I reached the top, and the downward side was steeper than I thought. By the time I neared the bottom, I was running so fast, I lost control of my legs and plowed into the sand. My knee hit on something hidden in the dirt and, when I got to my feet, the blood was running down my shin and into my moccasin. The way it squished between my toes bothered me something awful. I hopped on my good leg for a ways then limped on. I saw a couple of Indians watching me from the top of a nearby butte. I wondered if they were hoping I would fail the test. I topped the rise of a hill and saw a stream in the bottom of a narrow canyon. I hurried myself a little, figuring the cool water would give me some fresh energy. When I got to the bottom of the hill, I floundered into it, gulping great swallers of the cold water. It sure revived me in a hurry. I worked my way across and struggled up the bank on the other side. I lay there face-down for a few minutes, sucking in deep breaths of air until the burning in my lungs stopped. I rolled over and looked up at the sun. It was climbing fast into the sky. I got to my feet and took off at a fast run.

My leg was getting stiff from the cut in my knee, and it started to bleed again. My moccasins were so caked with mud and sand, my heels felt like they had rocks tied to them. I stopped long enough to jerk the moccasins off and fasten the strings together around my neck. It felt a lot better to run barefooted for a while.

When I came to the big gorge with cliffs rising high on both sides, it really spooked me. It didn't look like there was any possible way to get out of it, but this was the way Ashkea said I was to come. Trees and heavy undergrowth blocked my way. I had to get down on all fours to get through. When I stood up, I found myself in a prickly-pear field. I had a choice. I could go back the way I came or work my way through it. I decided to try my luck at going ahead. My moccasins were almost dry, and I sat down and put them on. I started through the spiny cactus bed, and the long thorns grabbed at my legs and wouldn't let go. They made deep scratches that started to bleed until the lower part of my legs were covered. I was sure glad when the bed thinned out to brush and scrub timber. I jerked as many thorns out of my moccasins and skin as I could, and my knees were shaking from hurrying so fast through the hot sun. The country began to spin around me, and I threw myself down under the nearest tree. I knew then I couldn't win this test alone. I called on God for help again.

"Please, God! I've got to make it. Don't let me give up!"

When my head cleared a little, I got to my feet and staggered on, and soon everything seemed all right again. I don't know how long it had been since I looked at the sun, but when I glanced up, it was at least three hours high. Ashkea's words still kept running through my mind: "... great warriors failed ... race the sun ... race the sun ..."

I was soon deep into the heart of the gorge, and it narrowed until it was only seventy-five or eighty feet wide. All at once, the sun was hidden by the ledges and towering rocks. I leaped from boulder to boulder until I found myself in a small pocket under a narrow, undercut ledge that circled like a horseshoe against the cliff rising above me. The gorge had dead-ended, and it was like I figured. There was no way out.

The ground was soft and moist, I guess, because the sun never reached it and, when I couldn't find a passage out, I climbed up on a big rock and looked around. Half hidden by the lip of the gorge, and probably twice as old as Cut Tongue, stood a tall, dead tree. Its long limbs reached out like skeleton arms toward a narrow ledge rimming the gorge. I studied the situation for a minute, then ran to the tree and climbed it. When I got three-fourths of the way up, I saw it was too far away from the ledge for me to reach it. I eased up on the tree a little higher and inched out on the stump of a broken limb that looked more solid than the rest. About that time, the tree started to shudder like it wanted to get rid of me. I couldn't figure out what was causing it until I looked down. My added weight to the dead roots was slowly pulling them from the soft ground. It was too far from the ledge for me to reach it, and I was going to have to go down with the tree. Something told me to get out as far on the broken limb as I could, and I

inched my way along it. All at once, the tree started
to lean with me in the direction of the ledge. It moved
close enough that I could get a good grip on some solid
rocks, and I pulled with all my might, guiding the tree
toward it. I glanced down at the ground and could see
the roots had nearly broken free. With a groan and
a heavy thud, the tree settled against the ledge's rim,
and I scrambled up to safety. I knew that once more,
I'd gotten the help I had asked for.

My eyes blurred in the bright sunshine as I
stumbled along the top of the high ridge. My body
was soaked with sweat, and I was so thirsty I could
have swallered a whole river. My head felt as light as
a ballon ready to drift off, and I glanced down at my
blood-covered body. My arms and legs were scratched
and bruised, my knee so badly swollen I could hardly
bend it. A yellow-like fluid oozed from the gash in it.

I was glad the ground had leveled off, and the
going was getting a lot easier. I looked first at the sun
then down at my shadow. It was short, and so was my
time!

I knew if I didn't get a drink of water soon, I
couldn't go on. I neared a low hill covered with trees
and brush. A high, mossed-over stone raised up behind an opening in the timber. Above it, another tree
spread out like an umbrella, and I could hear the
trickle of water. I cried out and stumbled to the small
spring that ran down a crevice in the moss-covered
rocks. I licked at the water with my swollen tongue
until my thirst felt better, then let it bubble over my
face and shoulders. I looked up at the sun, wondering
how much time I'd wasted, and Ashkea's voice came
to me again: ". . . Run like deer . . . Climb like lion . . .
Race the sun . . ."

I got to my feet and started out again. I was soon
on a trail that led to a rocky slope, then disappeared

against a high, jagged cliff that rose like it was climbing right up to the sky. I gasped when I looked above the rim of the cliff. The needle point of Crooked Sky shot upward just beyond. I was almost there! I looked the cliff up and down, then at the sun. I knew the hardest part of my test was yet to come and, if I was to make it, it would take me and God both!

Chapter Nineteen

Part of the time while I was climbing that cliff, I think I just swung by my fingertips. It was like my spirit had left my body and watched it struggle up the face of it. Once, when I looked down, I got so dizzy I almost fell, and I put my face against the wall so I couldn't see below. I gripped the niches and clefts with my fingers and toes, hanging with all of my strength until my arms and legs quivered and jerked so bad I was sure I would tumble back down. When I was almost ready to give up, I thought about Ma and Pa and what I must do so they could see Charlotte again. Somehow, it gave me strength to climb on.

I'd lost one of my moccasins, and the other was slashed to ribbons. The rocks gouged my feet, and my arms and shoulders ached from hanging on to that cliff. I had a hard time to find enough crevices to hold on to. Not a breath of air moved, and it seemed to me the hot sun was trying to scorch the life out of me so I would fail. At times, it all seemed like a bad dream, and I thought I'd sure wake up and find myself at home in my own bed. Ashkea's voice came again to me, ". . . Race the sun . . . Race the sun!" And it drove me on.

I took time to glance over my shoulder and up into the heavens. My time was running out! I almost shouted for joy when I pulled myself up on a narrow ledge and could stop long enough to draw a few deep breaths. I stood up on the close overhang, and almost immediately a heavy gust of wind came up. I think it figured to blow me off, but after I swayed back and forth a minute or two, I outsmarted it by hanging on to some rocks that were part of the cliff. When it died down, I inched along the ledge until I found a place to pull myself up higher. All at once, my fingers broke their hold and I slipped, losing my footing. I thought that was the end of me, and I'd land down at the bottom of the cliff. I grabbed a jutting rock to break my fall, then something rolled and bounced down the face of the cliff with a hollow sound. A quick glance made me shudder when I saw it was a dried human skull. I looked down at my feet resting on the bleached bones of a skelton, and that threw such a scare into me it didn't take me long to get out of there. I scrambled up to the next ledge like a dragon was on my tail, and didn't have a bit of trouble finding footholds.

When I ran clean out of breath, I had to rest a bit to cool my burning lungs. I looked at the sun. It was high noon. What a predicament to be in! I knew without a miracle I could never make it. My throat started to ache, and I shut my eyes to head off the tears.

"Please, God!" I begged. "Please don't let me fail now!"

In my hurry to get away from those dried bones, I lost my other moccasin. Both feet were bleeding, and the gash in my knee had opened up. The blood ran down my leg and between my toes, making the sole of my foot slippery. My strength was going fast, and I hugged the cliff with all I had to keep from falling. Just in time, I reached another slanting ledge that I could crawl along, and the world started spinning around me. It seemed like I was outside of my body again, and I thought I was tumbling through space. The feeling finally left, and I flattened down on my belly on the ledge so I wouldn't topple off.

"I can't make it, Charlotte!" I cried out in despair. "I can't! I can't!"

I soon got to feeling better, and stood up, edging along the shelf. It narrowed until I barely had anything to stand on. I clung to overhead rocks, frantically searching for a good handhold. I stretched higher and my fingers, topping the edge of the cliff, touched something. It was like God had put that long tree root in my hand! I guess the wind had blown it out of the dirt, and it was still fastened to the tree. It was frayed and barely hung over the edge of the cliff. I grabbed it like I would a rope and gave it a hard tug to see if it would hold me. It seemed solid enough, and I gripped it tight. With my feet flat against the cliff, hand over hand, I pulled myself over the top. Exhausted, I fell on the ground, sobbing helplessly, like every breath would be my last.

I wanted to die right there, and felt myself drifting off. Then a shrill cry broke through my mind and increased to a roar like thunder. I stumbled to my feet, realizing the Indians had sighted me from where they lined the trail, and it was their voices I heard. I moved forward in a daze. My vision was foggy, but I could see Crooked Sky still some distance away. Charlotte, her head covered and her back to Temkai, still stood on the sacrificial rock. Her shoulders drooped with despair. Temkai was a short distance from her, his bow in his hand. Shumeki, his face like the rocks he stood on, watched Temkai and Charlotte.

The roar of the Indians' voices rose and fell like the wail of a fiddle. I glanced at the sun, then staggered into a run. I tried to straighten out my steps and put some hurry into me, but nothing seemed to work right. My heart seemed to be the only thing that moved, and it pounded like hail on a rooftop.

"Sam Sutter! You crazy durn kid!" Russian's

voice came through to me, and I saw him trying to force himself through the crowd of Indians, waving his arms like crazy.

I ran on, and all at once the cheers died. Everything was so quiet, it was like the whole world stopped to see what would happen next. I felt as if I were moving in slow motion as I staggered past the line of Indians. I just had to make it! I couldn't fail when I was so near!

My eyes seemed to fog up, and I couldn't hardly see Temkai and Shumeki. Charlotte was now hidden from my sight. I saw Shumeki motion to Temkai, and he fit his arrow to his bow. I ran on, and as I got closer to Crooked Sky, I could see that the great rock's shadow all but uncovered the gold arrow. Charlotte came into my view, and only thirty feet or so separated her from Temkai. Shumeki raised his arm, and Temkai lifted his bow. The shadow of Crooked Sky completely uncovered the gold arrow, and I'll never forget how it blazed in the sun.

I strained forward with all of my strength as Shumeki's arm slashed down. In a daze, I saw Temkai throw his bow to the ground. Footsteps pounded behind me and, once more, I heard Russian's voice yelling out, "Git back here, ya crazy, dumb kid!"

With more strength than I thought possible, I leaped toward Charlotte just as Shumeki grabbed Temkai's bow from the ground, fit the arrow and drew back the string. Ashkea's voice came from far back in my mind, ". . . Meet the arrow . . . Meet the arrow . . . Meet the arrow!"

With my last bit of strength, I lunged. I seemed to hang in mid-air as I made that last final effort to meet the arrow meant for my sister. I heard the twang of the bow, the swish of the arrow flying through the air, then saw it sink deep in Charlotte's back. Her shoulders wrenched, and she writhed and twisted as her body sagged forward to tumble over the edge of the sacrificial rock into the chasm below.

A loud, moaning wail, like that of a wounded animal, came from me. I sank in despair over the glittering, gold arrow, sobbing out my misery and despair. All of a sudden, my strength left me and everything went black.

Chapter Twenty

I guess the hardest thing I've ever had to face in my life was going back to tell Ma and Pa about Charlotte.

Squaw winter, the cold time before Indian summer, had come and gone, and late autumn was all over the country before we got home. I was glad when Russian insisted he come along with me to the homestead.

Ma and Pa saw us coming and met us in the yard, and I'll never forget the joy and relief on their faces when they saw I was all right. Ma didn't scold me even once but just hugged me tight like she'd never let me go. Pa gripped my hand, then pulled me up against him and couldn't say a word. It wasn't until later the whole story came out about Charlotte. Russian looked up from a plate of Ma's beans and salt pork.

"It was the durndest, blood-thirstiest game I ever heerd of," he said. "Standin' thet poor, innocent daughter of yours out there on thet rock and expectin' a kid like Sam to race the sun outa that big canyon and up a granite wall. An' all for the privilege of receivin' an arrow that was meant for her. I tell ya, I've never seen a man with more guts than this boy!"

Russian bragging on me like that made me feel plenty foolish, and I ducked my head. When I looked up, Ma was wiping her eyes, and I knew how bad she must be hurting inside. Then Pa was at my side with his hand on my shoulder.

"I'm proud of you, son," he said, putting a grip in his fingers that let me know he meant every word of it. "Proud of your courage and unselfishness. Really does show how much you loved your sister, offerin' your life for her like you did."

When Pa talked to me like that, it made my throat get all full, and I swallered hard, not being able to say a word of thanks or anything. Then Ma came to me and really made the tears come, when she told me how proud she was, too. I buried my face in her shoulder, and her tears ran down on my cheek. I didn't take any shame in crying, feeling the warmth of her bosom, and knowing she really loved me and was glad I was back.

The next morning, the three of us watched Russian ride away. I knew it was going to be tough on him, going back to his place with old B'ar Killer gone. Before he got out of sight, he turned and waved. I waved back, then said, "There goes the best friend a feller ever had, Pa."

He nodded, and we both grinned when Russian's loud, tuneless singing drifted back to us. I knew then, no matter what, old Russian would always be all right.

Winter came and iced up the pond, and the call of wild geese flying south told us we could sure expect a hard one. The first snow fell early. That morning when Pa went to do chores, it covered the ground pretty deep. Ma worked over the stove preparing breakfast, and I was fooling around with a shaggy-haired pup that Milt Adams had given me . . . for coming home safe, he said. I had the pup doing roll-overs and all kinds of tricks. When he did them right, I scratched his belly and told him what a fine dog he was. He whined and whimpered to let me know how good it felt. I laughed at his antics, then all at once, he snapped at my hand. Just playing, I cuffed him a good one at the side of the head. He yipped like I'd half killed him and crawled under the chair to pout.

"What're you doin' with that dog?" asked Ma. "You ought to be out helpin' with the chores, 'stead of fiddlin' so much time away on him. Sometimes, I think it was a mistake for Milt to give him to you."

"He's sure smart, Ma," I said. "If I teach him right, he'll be a real good dog someday."

"Well, he's nothin' but a nuisance now," she said.

As if to prove it, the pup came out from under the chair and started chewing on one of Ma's bedroom slippers.

"Give that here, B'ar Killer," I said, taking the slipper away from him and setting him up on my lap.

"B'ar Killer?" said Ma. "Why do you want to give him a name like that?"

I rubbed the pup's ears, and he tried to lick my face. "I've got my reasons, Ma," I replied.

Pa came in right then, carrying the empty milk bucket. When he first opened the door, I knew something was wrong. He gave me a sharp look.

"Well, now . . ." he said, ". . . the cow's gone!"

I knew by his face I'd better wait for the rest.

"How many times do I have to tell you, Sam, to make shore that barn door's closed?"

"I thought I did," I said.

"What you think and what you do are two different things," he said, hanging his coat on a nail behind the door. He came over and sat down at the table, and Ma began to fill his plate with food. "Now, Mollie, we've had enough weeks of this mopin' around, and it's time we all git back to normal livin'."

Ma looked sort of startled, then he turned to me. "Git your breakfast eaten, Sam, then git out lookin' fer Callie."

I didn't do any arguing and got right to the task like he said. A bit later, I was follering Callie's tracks through the snow. They led off toward the hills, and I could see no reason for a cow to be taking out in the dead of winter when she had plenty of feed and a good warm barn to stay in. But then you never can tell about cows.

It wasn't long until I heard the tinkling of the bell around her neck. I looked around, but could see no sign of her. It came again from over the hill, and I took off at a run. I came up over the top and stopped dead. Callie was tied to some dry willows by the creek in the bottom of a draw, and a withered old Indian woman was trying to milk her in a strange-looking jar. Callie was having none of it and ran in circles around her, wild-eyed and plumb scared out of her wits. When the old woman got her slowed down enough to get up to her again, she kicked the jar out of her hand. The Indian screeched loud enough to put a flock of snowbirds to flight, and went to beating Callie on the ribs with her fists. I knew then it was time I took a hand.

When the old woman saw me coming, she backed up like she thought I was going to do something to her. I held up my hand in a friendly gesture, like I'd seen Russian do with the Indians, but she paid me no nevermind. She kept moving back like she was going to break and run. Then I heard the cry of a baby. I gazed around for it, then saw the form of another person lying in the snow wrapped in some dirty blankets, completely covered to keep out the snow. I figured it had to be another woman, because the crying came from a bundle beside her. I started toward them, and the old woman lost her scare and stepped in front of me, her eyes flashing, daring me to try to go past. You can bet I pulled up real fast, and she bent to pick up the baby that didn't seem old enough to me to be out in the storm. The one in the blanket didn't move, but I knew the baby had to be hers. I wondered if she was sick or dead, and started to go for a look. The old woman stepped in front of me again, but I was close enough then to tell by the way the blankets were moving up and down that she was breathing a little.

With gestures, I said, "I only want to help."

The old squaw looked at me like she didn't trust me at all, so I picked up the jar and went over to Callie. She stood real still while I milked into it. The Indian watched me all the while, and when I brought the jar over and handed it to her, she took it quick enough, and started to pour a little bit at a time into the baby's mouth. It stopped crying, but I knew then and there the three needed some help real bad. I took off my coat and handed it to the Indian woman, and she wrapped it around the baby. I pointed to the one on the ground and motioned toward our homestead.

"I'll go for help," I said, trying to let her know by the tone of my voice I meant no harm. "You just wait here."

I took off up the hill as hard as I could run.

Chapter Twenty-One

When I got home and told Pa about the Indian women, and asked for the team and wagon, he offered to come with me. I didn't know what to do about Ma. After what happened to Charlotte, I knew she'd have a fit if she guessed what we were up to. Pa said he could handle her when the time came and for me not to worry. I sure hoped he knew what he was talking about. I managed to slip into the house for a couple of blankets without Ma seeing me, then we headed out.

It was sometime later that Pa drove the wagon into our yard. I was on the seat beside him, and the old woman huddled beneath it in her blanket, the baby in her arms. Pa had wrapped the sick one up good in Ma's blanket and layed her in the wagon bed. Callie was fastened to the tailgate.

Pa squinted toward the cabin where a horse stood tied to the hitching rail.

"Looks like we got a visitor," he said.

"It's Russian!" I said, recognizing the old trapper's horse just as he and Ma stepped out of the cabin. "Do ya think Ma'll see fit to help 'em, Pa?"

"Like I said, you let me handle your ma, Sam."

He pulled the horses to a halt in front of the cabin.

"Howdy, Russian," I said, first giving Ma a quick glance. "How are ya?"

"Where've you two been so long?" cut in Ma. "Runnin' off without a word. I've been worried sick."

Pa ignored her. "What brings you out here in this storm, Habbakuk?" he asked Russian.

"It was about to get me locked in them mountains," said the trapper. "The damnedest blizzard I've seen back my way in many a y'ar. Hoped I might stay a spell with you folks 'til I see how things shape up."

Pa tied the horses to the brake handle and leaped to the ground. I followed him.

"Well, now, you're shore welcome to stay as long as you like." Pa turned to me. "Sam, take your cow to the barn."

I went to the back of the wagon to untie Callie.

"John, are you goin' to tell me where you two've been?" Ma demanded. "It didn't take both of you to bring that cow home."

"Mollie, we've got someone here that's mighty sick and needs your help," Pa said.

"Sick!" said Ma.

He motioned to the back of the wagon, and Ma moved toward it, Russian follering. Just as Ma looked in, the old squaw raised up out of her blankets with the baby in her arms. Ma sure gaped for a minute, then the blood rushed to her face and I could see she was shocked speechless and plenty full of mad. She turned to stare at Pa and me.

"Well," chuckled Russian, "look what you've brung home! Where'd you find 'em, John?"

"Down the country a ways," said Pa, trying to avoid Ma's hard look.

"There's another one that's awful sick lyin' in there," I put in, pointing to the bed of the wagon. "You've gotta help 'er, Ma!"

Ma looked like she was going to pop. "I ain't carin' for no sick Injun!" she snapped. "What do ya mean, bringin' 'em home to me when you know how I feel about 'em?"

"Now, Mollie," said Pa, trying to sooth her, "we couldn't just leave 'em out there to die. Think of that little baby, there."

"Well, if there's any doctorin' to be done, you'll have ta do it, and down in the barn, too, 'cause they ain't steppin' foot in my house!"

"Ma!" I gasped.

"I mean what I say!" The blood was really boiling in her face by this time.

Russian looked at Ma hard for a minute, like he couldn't believe her words. "Are my ears a' hearin' right, ma'am? You mean you'd let that little baby die . . . and that sick mother, without liftin' a finger, jest 'cause they're Injuns?"

Ma's look at Russian was plumb hostile. "After what they did to—to—" Her voice broke, and a strange expression passed over her face. Then it softened a little.

"Please, Ma," I pleaded. "Ya gotta help 'em."

"It's about time we put off all this hatin', Mollie," Pa said. "What's done's done. The important thing now is someone's sick and needs you."

The old Indian woman moved to the back of the wagon, the baby still in her arms, and started to get down. I reached for the baby. It gave me a chance to look at it real good. It sure was cute. After the woman had climbed out, I handed it back to her. Ma gazed at all of us a bit, then I could see her lower lip start to tremble and she went to the tailgate and leaned over the sick Indian woman. We all gathered around as she pulled back the blankets. Then she stood like she was froze as she stared at the small Bible clutched in the woman's thin hand. It was Charlotte's Bible! Ma grabbed the book and looked at it close, then jerked the blankets further back and peeled the crusted rags

116

from the woman's face. She went as white as a pan of Callie's milk and cried out.

"Father above! It's Charlotte!"

"Charlotte?" I rushed up to look.

"No! It can't be!" exclaimed Pa.

Russian stared. "It's a miracle, that's what it is!" he said. ". . . And then comin' all this way alone!"

"But she died!" I cried. "I *saw* her! I saw her *die!*"

Everyone looked at me like they didn't know what to believe. Right then, Charlotte started to mutter and we all bent to listen. Her eyes slowly opened, and she looked around at us and tried to smile. Then she spoke like it took all of the strength she had.

"Ash—kee—a. She—she—died—" Her voice trailed off, like the effort to speak was too much for her.

"It was her!" I gasped, her words finally getting through to me. I felt the tears stinging my eyes. "She—she gave her life for Charlotte . . . the greatest love anyone can have!"

I stared off in a daze, once again seeing in my mind the arrow flying from Shumeki's bow and sinking in Ashkea's back, then her body tumbling off the edge of the precipice. I shuddered. Russian put his arm around me, and I knew he felt for me. Ma clung to Charlotte's hand like she'd never let it go, sobbing all the while. Russian took the baby from the old squaw and handed him to Pa. They looked down at him for a moment.

"Ain't he a cute lil' feller?" said Russian.

Ma finally got hold of herself. "Let me have the baby, John," she said, "and help me get them inside."

Pa handed her the baby, and she gazed down at him with a look of love like I'd never seen on her face before. Pa lifted Charlotte from the wagon and follered Ma toward the house. The old Indian woman trailed behind, like she wasn't sure if she'd be welcome or not. When Ma opened the cabin door, my pup came tearing out like someone had set fire to his tail. He made a beeline for Russian and, first thing, went to chewing on his pants leg, snarling and growling like a hound would shake a skunk.

"What the hell—! Son of a—!" yowled Russian, trying to kick the pup loose. But the pup had his teeth locked, and hung on like he'd never let go.

I dashed over and pulled him off, then picked him up in my arms. Russian looked so mad for a second, I was sure he was going to swat us both a good one.

"I've been savin' him for you, Russian," I said. "His name's B'ar Killer."

Russian stared at me first, then the dog. He swallered hard, then all at once he flared. "You dumb kid! Don't you know better'n to give an ugly runt like him my dog's name?"

He yelled so loud, I ducked my head, feeling kind of hurt. I felt his eyes on me for a second or two, then he reached for the dog.

"Oh, well," he said, "give 'im here."

The pup went to licking his face, and a warm expression crossed the trapper's crusty old face. He looked at me out of the corner of his eye, trying not to show that he really was pleased. When he reached out and ruffled my hair, I was sure he liked the dog already. He turned and headed for the cabin, and I watched him for a minute before turning toward the barn with Callie.

I don't know what made me look up on the high ridge overlooking our homestead. I was startled to see Temkai sitting there on his horse like a statue. I knew he'd seen everything that had taken place when he raised his hand to me in farewell, then turned and rode out of sight over the hill.

ABOUT THE AUTHORS

ELEANOR LAMB, grandmother, mother of three and former wife of Nevada State Senator Floyd Lamb, is a rider, rancher, tennis player, store owner and writer. The film *Against a Crooked Sky* was inspired by one of her short stories, "The Tale of a Truant Cow." Ms. Lamb has also written a novel, *The Jim Savage,* and co-authored a musical screenplay, *Johnny Appleseed.* DOUGLAS STEWART, Ms. Lamb's nephew, is a screenwriter and co-owner of Omega Productions. In addition to the screenplay and novelization of *Against a Crooked Sky,* Ms. Lamb and Mr. Douglas have collaborated on two other screenplays, the award-winning *Where the Red Fern Grows* and *Seven Alone.*

READ YOUR WAY TO ADVENTURE

And share the joys and frustrations, triumphs and defeats of other young people.

☐ **DOWN THE LONG HILLS by Louis L'Amour**   2038 ● $1.25
Can a young boy and girl stranded all alone survive starvation, Indian raids, savage outlaws, and wild animals?

☐ **STAR TREK 10 by James Blish**   2241 ● $1.25
Spock views the forbidden Kollos and goes insane—and much more—in 6 new episodes from the TV series.

☐ **BAD FALL by Charles P. Crawford**   2459 ● 95¢
In this chilling tale of evil, a shy boy's friendship with a strange newcomer turns into a terrifying nightmare.

☐ **GIFTS OF AN EAGLE by Kent Durden**   8471 ● $1.25
The true story of a boy and the wil... he lived with for 16 years.

☐ **SUMMER OF MY GERMAN SOLDIER by Bette Greene** 8517 ● $1.25
A lonely Jewish girl forms a tragic friendship with a runaway prisoner of war.

☐ **OX GOES NORTH by John Ney**   8658 ● $1.25
He's fat and slow and very dangerous. This is one poor rich kid fortune hunters can't scare.

☐ **WHERE THE RED FERN GROWS by Wilson Rawls** 8676 ● $1.25
Billy loves his coon hounds and trains them to be champions, but tragedy lies ahead.

Buy them at your local bookstore or use this handy coupon for ordering:

REACH ACROSS THE GENERATIONS

With books that explore disenchantment and discovery, failure and conquest, and seek to bridge the gap between adolescence and adulthood.

☐ NOBODY WAVED GOODBY Elizabeth Haggard	2090 •	$ .95
☐ PHOEBE Patricia Dizenzo	2104 •	$ .95
☐ IT'S NOT THE END OF THE WORLD Judy Blume	2764 •	$ .95
☐ DAVE'S SONG Robert McKay	2893 •	$1.25
☐ THE BELL JAR Sylvia Plath	6400 •	$1.75
☐ I KNOW WHY THE CAGED BIRD SINGS Maya Angelou	6478 •	$1.50
☐ RUN SOFTLY, GO FAST Barbara Wersba	7343 •	$ .95
☐ THE MAN WITHOUT A FACE Isabelle Holland	7804 •	$ .95
☐ THE UPSTAIRS ROOM Reiss	7818 •	$ .95
☐ I NEVER LOVED YOU Paul Zindel	7993 •	$ .95
☐ BONNIE JO, GO HOME nette Eyerly	8030 •	$ .95
☐ MY DARLING, MY HAMBURGER Paul Zindel	8172 •	$ .95
☐ RICHIE Thomas Thompson	8327 •	$1.50
☐ HATTER FOX Marilyn Harris	8395 •	$1.50
☐ SUMMER OF MY GERMAN SOLDIER Bette Greene	8517 •	$1.25
☐ THE FRIENDS Rosa Guy	8541 •	$1.25
☐ OX GOES NORTH John Ney	8658 •	$1.25
☐ WHERE THE RED FERN GROWS Wilson Rawls	8676 •	$1.25
☐ ELLEN: A SHORT LIFE, LONG REMEMBERED Rose Levit	8729 •	$1.25

Buy them at your local bookstore or use this handy coupon for ordering:

Bantam Books, Inc., Dept. EDN, 414 East Golf Road, Des Plaines, Ill. 60016

Please send me the books I have checked above. I am enclosing $_____ (please add 35¢ to cover postage and handling). Send check or money order —no cash or C.O.D.'s please.

Mr/Mrs/Miss_____

Address_____

City_____State/Zip_____

EDN—4/76

Please allow three weeks for delivery. This offer expires 4/77.